Flight
—of the—
Fugitives

Trailblazer Books

TITLE	HISTORIC CHARACTERS
Attack in the Rye Grass	Marcus & Narcissa Whitman
The Bandit of Ashley Downs	George Müller
The Betrayer's Fortune	Menno Simons
The Chimney Sweep's Ransom	John Wesley
Escape from the Slave Traders	David Livingstone
Flight of the Fugitives	Gladys Aylward
The Hidden Jewel	Amy Carmichael
Imprisoned in the Golden City	Adoniram and Ann Judson
Kidnapped by River Rats	William & Catherine Booth
Listen for the Whippoorwill	Harriet Tubman
The Queen's Smuggler	William Tyndale
Shanghaied to China	Hudson Taylor
Spy for the Night Riders	Doctor Martin Luther
Trial by Poison	Mary Slessor

Flight
—of the—
Fugitives

DAVE & NETA JACKSON
Text Illustrations by
Julian Jackson

BETHANY HOUSE PUBLISHERS
MINNEAPOLIS, MINNESOTA 55438

Inside illustrations by Julian Jackson.
Cover design and illustration by Catherine Reishus McLaughlin.

Published by Bethany House Publishers
A Ministry of Bethany Fellowship, Inc.
11300 Hampshire Avenue South
Minneapolis, Minnesota 55438

Printed in the United States of America

Library of Congress Cataloging-in-Publication Data

Jackson, Dave, 1944–
    Flight of the fugitives / Dave and Neta Jackson ; text
illustrations by Julian Jackson.
       p. cm. (Trailblazer books ; #13)
    Summary: After coming to China to work as a missionary in the
early 1930's, Gladys Aylward adopts several orphans and tries to
save nearly a hundred more during the war between China and
Japan.

    1. Aylward, Gladys—Juvenile fiction. [1. Aylward, Gladys—
Fiction. 2. Missionaries—Fiction. 3. Orphans—Fiction. 4.
China—History—1937–1945—Fiction. 5. Christian life—Fiction.]
I. Jackson, Neta. II. Jackson, Julian, ill. III. Title. IV. Series.
PZ7.J132418F1   1994
[Fic]—dc20   94–32699
ISBN 1–55661–466–7   CIP
                                             AC

All the characters and major events in this book are real. However, the war events of 1938–1940 have been condensed for the sake of the story. For instance, Feng was not released to Gladys Aylward's care until 1939, the second time the people of Yangcheng fled to Bei Chai Chuang.

Also, Gladys Aylward met Colonel Linnan during the war, not at Yangcheng, but at the Christian Mission in Tsehchow. His earlier role in the arrest of Ninepence's uncle is purely fiction.

Probably Gladys Aylward's adopted children were not invited to the Mandarin's farewell dinner; they are included here to preserve the story's "point-of-view."

The one hundred children she took over the mountains were actually from the mission in Tsehchow; also, it is not known if Feng made the trip over the mountains with Gladys, although he stayed with her for many years.

Gladys Aylward had five adopted children, only three of whom are highlighted in this story.

DAVE AND NETA JACKSON are a husband/wife writing team who have authored or coauthored many books on marriage and family, the church, and relationships, including the books accompanying the Secret Adventures video series, the Pet Parables series, and the Caring Parent series.

They have three children: Julian, the illustrator for the Trailblazer series, Rachel, a college student, and Samantha, their Cambodian foster daughter. They make their home in Evanston, Illinois, where they are active members of Reba Place Church.

CONTENTS

Chapter 1

Gypsy Woman

MEI-EN CLUNG DESPERATELY to her stepfather's back as he clambered over the rocky path leading to the next town. If she let go, she might tumble down the mountainside and land on the jagged rocks far below.

But that worry was like a tiny millet seed compared to the big lump of fear growing inside the six-year-old's stomach. Where was her stepfather taking her? Why was he so angry?

Mei-en held on tightly and squeezed her eyes

shut so she didn't have to look at the steep mountainside falling away below them. But when she closed her eyes, her mind saw the earth being shoveled on top of the crude wooden coffin that held the body of her mother. Hot tears filled her eyes as she remembered trying to wake up her mother just that morning. . . .

"Mama! Mama-san!" she had cried, shaking the still form of her mother, who was lying on the flat, brick stove where the little family slept each night to keep warm. For two weeks, her mother had been coughing and feverish, barely able to cook the millet mush and thin, watery soup they ate each day. But that morning her mother didn't wake up.

Her stepfather was angry. Without saying anything to Mei-en, he built the coffin, dug the hole in a field outside their mountain village, and sent for the Buddhist priest. As soon as the incense had been burned and the burial rites performed, he had grabbed six-year-old Mei-en and started up the mountain.

"Get down . . . get down!" she heard her stepfather say, shaking her loose. Mei-en opened her eyes, slid off his back, and crumpled gratefully to the ground beside the path. A rest at last. The little girl was very thirsty, but so far they had not passed any creeks flowing down the mountainside.

"No, no! Get up!" scolded her stepfather. "You are too heavy . . . walk! Walk!" And he set off again along the rocky path.

Mei-en scrambled to her feet, which were bound

tightly in long strips of cloths, trying to ignore the sharp pain that shot up both legs as she stumbled along the path. Her feet *always* hurt, but she did not dare say anything about it. That was the unspoken rule. Chinese girls who wished to have beautiful, tiny feet when they grew up must not complain about having their feet bound.

But the pain made it impossible to keep up with her stepfather, who was hiking up the trail at a swift pace. Mei-en hobbled along on her tiny feet, falling frequently, until once, when she looked up, she could no longer see her stepfather.

"Papa!" she called out, feeling the fear in her stomach twist and knot. "Papa-san! Come back!"

For a moment all she heard was the sound of her own voice bouncing back from the mountainside. Then her stepfather reappeared, a frown clouding his thin face.

"Worthless girl!" he muttered, picking her up and slinging her on his back once more.

The man with the girl on his back, their dark blue trousers and dark blue shirts dusty from the long walk, plodded into town as the afternoon sun was sliding down behind the mountains. Mei-en peeked over her stepfather's shoulder. The houses along the street looked vaguely familiar, but she couldn't remember why.

Her stepfather turned into a courtyard in front of

a large, wooden-beamed house with a curved, red-tiled roof and decorated paper windows that slid open and shut. As he rang the bell inside the courtyard, the sound jangled in Mei-en's memory. . . .

Now she remembered! This was her grandmother's house—her real father's mother.

Before she had a chance to wonder why they were there, the door of the house swung open and a middle-aged woman with a round, wrinkled face appeared, her black hair streaked with gray and pulled back into a bun at the nape of her neck.

The woman's eyes darted from the man to the little girl swaying with weariness beside him, then back to the man.

"What are you doing here?" the woman spat out angrily. "I paid you money. You promised I would not see you again!"

The man's lip curled. "It was a bad bargain, Mrs. Chou. When your son died, I agreed to marry your daughter-in-law and take her worthless girl child off your hands because you promised the woman would give me sons." He laughed hollowly. "She has given me nothing but two dead babies."

"What hap—?"

"Dead," said Mei-en's stepfather angrily. "Pneumonia. I buried her this morning. Now I have brought her child back to you."

The woman's jaw clenched. "But we agreed!"

"The agreement is off!" shouted the man. "This is your son's child! Can I help it if he was so foolish as to fall down the mountain and get killed? Now her mother is dead also. *You* are her blood relative—not me."

The lump in Mei-en's stomach tightened and her heart pounded. She only vaguely remembered her real father, but many times she had dreamed about him. In her dreams he was a handsome Chinese man, with golden tan skin and jet black hair, laughing almond-shaped eyes, white teeth, and strong shoulders. She dreamed that he held her in his arms . . . that he talked to her and laughed. . . .

"Come back here!" yelled her grandmother's shrill voice.

Mei-en jerked her head around and saw the back of her stepfather disappearing through the courtyard gate. Slowly she turned back and looked up into her grandmother's face.

Mrs. Chou, fists planted on her hips, looked down at the little girl. "By the gods, I am not going to be stuck with a worthless girl child," she muttered angrily. With that, the woman went back inside and slammed the heavy wooden door.

Instinctively, Mei-en ran on her bound feet to the gate and looked up and down the street. Farmers were coming in from their fields on the mountainsides . . . women were balancing straw baskets on poles across their shoulders . . . a stray dog stood in the middle of the road and barked at no one in particular. But there was no sign of her stepfather.

Mei-en just stood in the gate, shivering as the shadows lengthened and the brief warmth of the mountain spring faded with the light. What was she going to do? Her mother was dead . . . her stepfather didn't want her . . . her honorable grandmother didn't want her, either.

Sinking to the ground, Mei-en could no longer hold back the tears. Sobs shook her little body as she wrapped her thin arms around her legs, put her head down on her knees, and cried.

Mei-en had been crying for a long time when she sensed someone standing nearby. Startled, she looked up. A strange woman was standing a few feet away, staring at her. The daylight was almost gone, but Mei-en could see that the woman's clothes were not the plain, blue shirt and trousers worn by most of the men and women in the mountain villages of Shansi Province. Instead, she wore several layers of clothes, topped by a dirty, red and yellow skirt that hung to her ankles. Her hair was covered by a cloth turban, framing a leathery, wrinkled face; silver earrings dangled from her ears, and her bare wrists and ankles were covered by rows of silver bangles.

Mei-en's mouth dropped open. She had never seen such a strange sight in her whole life.

"Why are you crying, girl?" the woman said, not unpleasantly.

Mei-en hid her face. A young girl was not supposed to talk to strangers.

"What business is it of yours, gypsy?" demanded another voice. Mrs. Chou suddenly appeared in the open gate, hands planted on her hips.

The stranger's leathery face wrinkled into a smile, revealing blackened, decayed teeth. "I was just wondering who this child belongs to," the gypsy said.

14

"Night is falling . . . she is sitting alone in the gate . . . maybe she is lost . . . ?"

Mei-en wanted her grandmother to say, "She belongs to me! Now go away." But instead she heard her grandmother say slowly, "Why do you want to know?"

The stranger's voice became syrupy. "Well . . . a young girl might be useful to me . . . but of course, taking care of a child is a lot of bother . . . so I'm not sure it would be worth it, unless . . ."

Mei-en scrambled to her feet and looked pleadingly into her grandmother's face. She did not want to go with this woman! She would be quiet . . . she would not be any trouble . . . she would learn how to cook and sew and clean for her grandmother. . . .

Her grandmother ignored her. "How much do you want?" she asked bluntly.

"Oh . . . two hundred *cash* would buy food and lodging for me and the child for several weeks," said the woman, grinning.

"Two hundred *cash*! A whole dollar?" screamed the grandmother. "That's robbery! I won't do it! This child has already cost me good money, and I'm not about to pay again."

The gypsy woman shrugged and picked up a big bundle sitting by her feet. "Oh, well. I just thought I'd ask." And the woman turned to go.

"Wait!" said Mrs. Chou. "I will give you one hundred *cash*—half a dollar—to take the girl. It is a bargain . . . I know you will sell her to the Mandarin in some town, or to a poor family looking for a bride for their son. Either way, you will make money off this deal. Take it or leave it."

The woman brightened. "I will take it. Come, come," she said, holding out a clawlike hand, "let's be done with it."

Trembling, Mei-en watched as her grandmother fished under her cloth jacket and pulled several coins from a hidden pocket.

"Here," she said, placing them in the gypsy's outstretched hand. "But if I ever see you or the girl again, I will call the police and have you arrested for child-stealing!"

The stranger grinned again, revealing her rotten teeth. "Do not worry, Honorable Grandmother," she said in her slippery voice. "We shall be gone from this place. Come, girl."

With that, Mei-en felt the clawlike hand grab the scruff of her blue jacket, nearly jerking her off her feet, and pull her out into the darkening street.

Chapter 2

Foreign Devil

T HE MAIN STREET OF YANGCHENG was crowded with food sellers, market goers, and mule drivers and their beasts wending their way through the mountain city. People hurried past the haggard-looking gypsy woman squatting beside the roadway bleating, "Can you spare a penny for the poor?" . . . and hardly anyone noticed the thin, six-year-old lying in the dirt at her feet.

Mei-en was so hungry she could hardly think of anything but food. It had been two days since she had eaten anything . . . and weeks since her belly had been really full. She had lost count of how many villages they wandered through, begging for food and money, or how many times they had slept out in the open on the hard ground. Sometimes the gypsy woman had tried to sell Mei-en to the mayor of a town or some other prominent citizen, but no one was interested in the thin little waif.

And so finally they had set out for Yangcheng, the largest town in the area—a small, walled city, really—perched in the saddle between two mountains, a convenient stopping place for the mule trains that carried food and cooking pots and cloth and building materials and news from place to place. Even though the year was 1934, there were no roads in this mountainous part of northern China; no buses, no trains—only mule tracks threading their way through the mountains, connecting the little villages and walled towns like a single lifeline.

Mei-en had never been in a town as big as Yangcheng . . . but right now she didn't care. Her tightly bound feet throbbed from the weeks of walking; her stomach pinched with hunger. But even worse than the ache in her belly was the thirst. The noontime sun beat down on her dirty, itchy skin; her lips were dry and cracked, but when she tried to lick them, her tongue felt dry and thick.

Every now and then she heard a *clink* as someone threw a penny into the gypsy woman's bowl. But Mei-en knew that if there weren't enough pennies to feed the two of them, the woman would eat and she would go hungry another night.

Mei-en closed her eyes, her cheek on the dirt, the

loud noises of the street market drifting in and out of her consciousness. Then she heard a new sound . . . someone talking close by. . . .

"You there, beggar woman," a voice was saying. Mei-en's eyes fluttered open. The shadow of a person stood between her and the glaring sun. The shape looked like a woman, short, like other Chinese women . . . but there was something strange about her voice.

"Why do you let your child lie bareheaded in the street, with no hat to protect her from the sun?" the voice demanded. "She will get sunstroke! She may even die!"

The gypsy woman sighed. "So she dies . . . at least then I wouldn't have to feed her."

"You wicked woman!" the person cried. "Don't you have any compassion for your own child?"

The gypsy woman just shrugged. "If you care so much about her, why don't you buy her? I will sell her to you for . . . two hundred *cash*."

"Two hundred—!" the voice gasped. "I—I do not have that much money."

"What?" sneered the gypsy. "A foreign devil like yourself has no money? We know you English are all rich."

Foreign devil? Mei-en struggled to sit up, squinting against the sun. Once again her heart was pounding, the stab of fear in her chest making her momentarily forget the ache in her belly. She didn't want to be sold to a foreign devil! She would run . . . she would—

"Here," said the foreign woman, digging in the

pocket of her blue trousers and holding out a few coins to the gypsy. "This is all I have. Take it . . . and I will take the girl."

"*Ninepence?*" scoffed the gypsy. "I paid half a dollar for the brat myself. I can't afford to—"

"Take it!" demanded the woman, shoving the coins into the gypsy's hands. "If you don't, the child may die, and then you would get nothing!"

The gypsy woman considered a moment, then got to her feet and within seconds had disappeared among the crowded market stalls, leaving Mei-en behind.

The next thing Mei-en knew, she was being lifted in the strange woman's arms. The little girl stared into the woman's face—and saw round, dark eyes in a pale, white face looking back at her. The woman really was a foreign devil dressed in Chinese clothes!

No . . . no! she tried to scream, but only grunts came from her parched mouth. She struggled in the woman's arms, but she was so weak with hunger and exhaustion that her efforts made no difference.

The foreign devil carried Mei-en through first one crowded street, then another. Then the woman turned into a large courtyard and cried out, "Yang? Yang! Come quickly!"

By this time, Mei-en was shaking with fright. Was the foreign devil going to boil her in a pot and eat her? From somewhere she found a surge of strength and began beating on the woman with her fists.

Surprised, the woman set her down. Suddenly

free, Mei-en scrabbled, crablike, into a corner of the courtyard behind a big urn full of blooming flowers. Just then an elderly Chinese man in blue shirt and trousers appeared from the big house, which looked like some kind of inn. It was two stories tall, with a red-tiled roof, and a stable on one end.

"Yang, talk to her," said the woman anxiously. "Tell her not to be afraid . . . that I want to help her."

The man named Yang looked toward Mei-en, who was half hidden behind the big urn. Then a big smile widened his face.

"No, not talk, Miss Gladys," he chuckled, and disappeared inside the house. In a moment he was back again, carrying a bowl of hot, steaming liquid. As he approached, Mei-en gave a rasping cry and tried to crawl farther behind the urn. But Yang simply set the bowl down on the ground; then he took the woman by the arm and went back inside.

Mei-en was alone in the courtyard. The bowl of soup was just out of her reach. She stared at the bowl, afraid of what might happen if she touched it. Was it poison? Were they trying to kill her?

But, she reasoned to herself, if she didn't drink it, she was going to die of thirst anyway. Having figured that out, the little girl crawled from behind the urn and picked up the bowl in trembling fingers. Raising it to her lips, she trickled the warm broth into her mouth. She swallowed with difficulty . . . then trickled more broth into her mouth.

Finally the bowl was empty. With a sigh, Mei-en crawled back behind the urn and fell fast asleep.

❖ ❖ ❖ ❖

When Mei-en woke a few hours later, the afternoon sun was shimmering on top of the red-tiled roof. She peeked out from behind the urn . . . and there on the ground sat the same bowl. But instead of being empty, it was now filled with boiled millet mush and a smattering of steamed vegetables on top.

The little girl looked around. The courtyard was empty. Crawling over to the bowl, she stuck her fingers into the food, then stuffed a handful of millet and vegetables into her mouth.

Mei-en's dry, cracked lips started to bleed as she chewed, but she kept eating until the bowl was empty. Sucking the last taste off her fingers, she looked up . . . and saw the old Chinese man and the foreign devil woman standing in the courtyard looking at her.

Panicking, Mei-en tried to crawl back behind the urn, but the old man was too fast for her. He picked her up and, holding her tightly as she kicked and struggled, sat down on a stone bench against the courtyard wall.

The food had revived Mei-en, and her screams echoed off the courtyard walls. But Yang just held her and began to hum, swaying gently on the bench and crooning soothing sounds in her ear. Soon the little girl quit struggling, but her eyes were wide with fright.

When Mei-en was quiet, the foreign woman approached and knelt in front of the old man and the girl. "Don't be afraid . . . I'm not going to hurt you," she murmured quietly, tucking her short, dark brown hair behind her ear.

And then the woman did something very strange. She took off the threadbare, cloth shoes Mei-en was wearing, and began to unwind the binding cloths from the little girl's feet. Frightened, Mei-en began to scream and struggle once more, but Yang just held her firmly and hummed soothing tunes in her ear.

"It's okay . . . it's all right," murmured the woman. "I'm the official Foot Inspector for Yangcheng and the whole district of Shansi . . . the Nationalist government wants all Chinese girls to have their feet unbound . . . yes, yes . . . it's okay . . . it's all right . . ."

The woman kept unwinding and unwinding . . . until one ashen little foot was naked. Mei-en gave a little cry—she couldn't remember the last time she had actually seen her bare feet. The toes were bent under and the whole foot seemed misshapen.

"Oh . . . oh," the woman said, looking genuinely distressed, "look at this poor foot. Never again will it be imprisoned by those horrible binding cloths." And slowly, gently, she began to massage the little foot.

As Mei-en's fear subsided, she was aware of a new sensation: tingling pain in her foot as the blood began to circulate under the gentle rubbing. The little girl started to wail.

"That's okay . . . go ahead and cry . . . I know it hurts, but it'll feel better soon . . . that's all right,"

murmured the woman as she continued to massage each little toe.

Then the unbinding of the other foot began . . . then the gentle rubbing . . . then the pain and tears . . .

Sniffling, the little girl watched the foreign woman's fingers gently waking up each toe. She stared at the short, dark hair—brown, not black—and plain white face. *Do all English have such big noses?* she wondered. *Not nice, flat noses like the Chinese.* But mostly she looked at the woman's eyes . . . eyes that seemed soft and kind.

Suddenly Mei-en burst into tears again, burying her face in the old man's chest and sobbing as if her heart would break.

But this time her tears weren't because of the pain. No one had touched her this gently and lovingly since that horrible day when her mother died.

Chapter 3

Inn of Eight Happinesses

THREE TIMES A DAY, the Englishwoman—whom Yang called Miss Gladys—bathed Mei-en's feet in warm water and then massaged the poor, bent toes. But when the woman asked the little girl what her name was, Mei-en just hung her head shyly.

"Well, then," smiled Gladys, "we'll call you Ninepence for now . . . how lucky I was to have ninepence in my pocket the day I found you!"

The nickname stuck. "Look how much soup Ninepence ate today!" Yang crowed happily the next day, holding up the little girl's empty bowl. And, "Show me how you can walk across the courtyard, Ninepence," Gladys urged her gently.

Soon the little girl was hobbling about, watching Yang cook up big pots of sticky millet mush, dough strings, and vegetable broth to serve to the mule drivers who stopped at their inn. Except . . . not many mule teams wanted to stop at an inn run by a "foreign devil," even if the cheerful sign over the gate did say "Inn of Eight Happinesses."

"You see," Yang explained patiently to Ninepence one day as he plucked a scrawny chicken to flavor a pot of soup, "not long ago there were *two* English ladies in Yangcheng. First came Mrs. Lawson . . . she had been in China a long, long time as a Christian missionary."

Ninepence wondered what a "missionary" was, but she didn't want to interrupt Yang's story.

"But when Mrs. Lawson came to Yangcheng," Yang continued, "nobody wanted to listen to a 'foreign devil' talk about her Christian God. So . . ." Yang beamed as he looked around the large inn, with its three brick *k'angs* for sleeping. "Mrs. Lawson bought this old inn . . . oh! it was a mess! Too much work for old Mrs. Lawson and old Yang. So Gladys Aylward came all the way from England to be Mrs. Lawson's helper. But . . . a few months ago Mrs. Lawson had an accident . . ."

Ninepence noticed that Yang's eyes suddenly filled with tears as he jerked feathers out of the limp chicken. But soon the old Chinese cook found his voice again and said, "So . . . it's just me and Miss Gladys now." His wide grin returned. "She speaks Chinese pretty good, yes? That's because *I* teach her."

In a daily effort to attract the reluctant mule drivers to stop at her inn, Gladys Aylward scrubbed every inch of the floors, laid fresh straw in the stable for the mules, and watered the flowers in the big urns so that the courtyard would look cheerful and appealing to the weary travelers. Then, toward evening, as the mule trains began drifting into the city, she would throw open the gate and call out, "*Muyo beatcha!* We have no bugs! *Muyo goodso!* We have no fleas!" Then the small Englishwoman would beckon eagerly toward the courtyard. "*Lai-lai-lai,*" she called. "Come, come, come."

But after several days had passed, and all the mule drivers had hurried by when they saw the "foreign devil," Ninepence heard Gladys mutter to herself, "Okay, if they want to be stubborn, stubborn can work two ways."

That evening, Gladys brought an armload of fresh hay into the courtyard. Then she threw open the courtyard gate and waited for the mule trains. As the first mules came clop, clop, clopping down the hard-packed dirt street, she called out as usual, "*Muyo beatcha!* We have no bugs! . . . *Muyo goodso!* We have no fleas! . . . *Lai-lai-lai!* Come, come, come!"

But when the mule driver started to hurry past, the Englishwoman lunged for the halter of the lead mule and, pulling with all her might, swung the animal's head toward the gate. Maybe it was the weight of the small woman hanging onto its halter . . . or maybe it was the smell of fresh hay . . . but within moments the mule had trotted into the court-yard, and behind it came all the rest of the mules in the mule train, who soon had their heads buried in the sweet-smelling hay.

Ninepence thought this was very funny. She hopped up and down, clapping her hands. *"How-how-how!"* she cried. "Good, good, good!"

Gladys Aylward gave the little girl a startled look. These were the first words Ninepence had spo-ken since she arrived several days earlier!

Meanwhile, the mule drivers were frantic. All their mules and packs were inside the courtyard of the "foreign devil" woman! They rushed into the courtyard and tried to pull the mules out again, but once the tired mules had stopped and tasted a mouth-ful of fresh hay, there was no way they were going to budge.

The mule drivers whispered anxiously among themselves outside the gate then reluctantly agreed to spend the night at the Inn of Eight Happinesses. After all, they reasoned, there were four of them and only one foreign devil, an old man, and a girl child.

When the men had pulled the heavy packs off their tired animals and bedded them down in the stable, they edged into the main room of the inn, all bunched together and looking about cautiously. It was one thing to meet a foreign devil out on the street; it was another to sleep in her house!

But Yang had bowls of dough strings smothered with chicken and vegetable broth waiting for them. Ninepence, who was still a little unsteady on her deformed feet, tried to help by passing out chopsticks and cups of tea. Then, while the men were eating hungrily, Gladys Aylward brought in a stool and sat down facing them. The men stopped chewing and looked uneasily at one another. What was the foreign devil woman going to do now?

"A long, long time ago in a land called Palestine," Gladys began, smiling at the rugged mule drivers, "some sheepherders were taking care of a herd of sheep . . ."

The men seemed to relax. A story? Well . . . a story wouldn't hurt anything.

"One night while they were sleeping out in the field with their sheep," Gladys continued, "a bright light woke them up. It was an angel from heaven with a message for them. 'God's Son has been born in a town nearby called Bethlehem,' the angel told them. 'This baby's name is Jesus, and He will become the Savior for all people everywhere.' Then many more angels filled the sky, singing, 'Glory to God in the Highest! Peace on earth to all people!' "

Ninepence sat cross-legged on the floor where no one would notice her, listening.

"After the angels left, the sheepherders were very excited!" said Gladys. "They had been waiting for this Savior to come for many, many years. And now He had been born! But would mere sheepherders be allowed to see such an important baby?"

32

The mule drivers murmured and nodded their heads. They were thinking the same question.

Gladys continued her story. "But they followed the angel's instructions and hurried into Bethlehem . . . and there they found the baby's parents in a stable and the baby lying in a bed of straw—just like the angel had told them! The sheepherders were surprised. They expected rich, important people, but this family looked like tired peasants who had been traveling for many days."

Smiles broke out on the faces of the mule drivers. This story was about people like themselves!

Ninepence thought the story was finished . . . but then Gladys told about three rich kings from another country who also came to visit this special baby, following a special star in the sky, and how the king of the baby's country felt threatened and tried to kill Him . . . but an angel warned the baby's parents in time, and they ran away to another country until the bad king died.

When the story was over, the mule drivers seemed pleased, and curled up on the warm, brick *k'angs* to sleep as Ninepence gathered up the dirty bowls.

"Did you like that story?" Yang asked her, showing the little girl how to wash the bowls. "That story came from a book called the Bible, which is full of wonderful stories about the Christian God."

Ninepence *did* like the story . . . though she didn't really understand it. That night, as she slept on the little pallet beside Gladys Aylward's bed in a tiny room upstairs, she dreamed of babies living in stables and kings riding on mules chasing angels over the mountains.

The next night, Gladys tried her "method" of dragging in the lead mule on another mule train . . . and this time during supper, she told the grumpy mule drivers a "long ago" story about a man named Noah. "God in heaven," said Gladys, "told Noah to build a big, big boat, big enough to hold a male and female of all the different animals. Everybody thought he was crazy . . . but then one day it began to rain. It rained and rained until the whole world was flooded."

The mule drivers nodded and murmured. They knew about flooding. Didn't the Yellow River on the other side of the mountains flood now and then and wipe out whole villages?

"Of course, all the wicked people drowned," Gladys went on, "everybody except Noah and his family and the animals in the boat, of course. And when the rain was over, God put a rainbow in the sky as a promise that He would never flood the whole earth ever again."

Ninepence couldn't wait until the next night to find out what the next story was going to be. Neither could the mule drivers, it seemed. Word began to go up and down the mule track about the Inn of Eight Happinesses in Yangcheng, where you could get a clean stable for your mules, good food, *and* an amazing story during supper for just a few *cash*.

By the end of summer, the three brick *k'angs* were full of mule drivers listening to Gladys's stories, which made the Englishwoman very happy. Even though Ninepence was only six, she finally figured out that a "missionary" must be somebody who liked to tell stories about the Christian God from a fat book called the Bible.

Unfortunately, the few *cash* Gladys charged to stay at the Inn of Eight Happinesses barely covered her expenses for food, hay, and straw.

"I must take another trip to the mountain villages as official Foot Inspector for the Mandarin," Gladys told Yang one day. "It is the only way to earn more income . . . and winter is coming, and we need warm clothes for Ninepence."

Ninepence was alarmed. Gladys was going away? What if she fell down the mountain as her father had done? Or got killed by bandits? Who would take care of her then?

"Please take me with you!" the little girl begged. "I will be good and not cause you any trouble."

Gladys smiled and squatted down beside Ninepence. "Of course you wouldn't cause me any trouble!" she said. "But . . . your feet are not yet strong enough for a mountain journey. Maybe next year."

She gently stroked Ninepence's sad face. "Besides, who would help Yang if we both went away?"

Chapter 4

Less Gets More

THE NEXT DAY NINEPENCE WATCHED sadly as Gladys rode off on the Mandarin's mule, accompanied by two of the Mandarin's soldiers . . . just in case the stubborn villagers didn't want to obey the new law about unbinding feet. Ninepence wiggled her own toes, which now stuck out nice and straight and no longer looked deformed, even though her feet still ached by the end of the day.

"Well, don't just stand there, Ninepence," scolded

Yang, hurrying back into the inn. "We have a lot of work to do while Miss Gladys is gone."

Yang said he was too old to clean out the stable, so he hired his brother-in-law's great-nephew to do the dirty work, but Ninepence offered to lay down the clean, fresh straw on the floor and fill the feed boxes with hay.

When she came into the inn, Yang was stirring his pots and muttering to himself, so Ninepence decided to wash the tops of the brick *k'angs* to discourage bugs, and stuck new coal into the warming stoves underneath to keep the fires burning.

When the sun started to slide down behind the mountains, Ninepence ran to the gate, swung it wide open and called out, "*Muyo beatcha!* We have no bugs! . . . *Muyo goodso!* We have no fleas! . . . *Lai-lai-lai!* Come, come, come!"

The first mule train plodded on by, without giving the Inn of Eight Happinesses a second glance. Ninepence was worried. Would she have to grab the halter of the lead mule, as Gladys sometimes did? She wasn't sure she could reach that high! But fortunately, the next mule train was being driven by a former customer, who herded his mules into the courtyard and began pulling off their packs.

Soon the *k'angs* were full of seated men, eagerly shoving dough strings and vegetables into their mouths. But as she served the tea, Ninepence suddenly felt alarmed. The story! Who would tell the story since Gladys was gone?

But just then Yang came out of the kitchen, wiping his hands on the big white towel he wore as an apron. The old man pulled up the stool, sat down, and began.

"A long, long time ago, there was a man named Noah," he said, smiling widely. "God told him to build a big boat and put animals inside because a big storm was coming. During the storm, Jesus came walking on the water up to the boat. Noah thought it was a ghost! But Jesus just knocked and said, 'Let me in, Noah.' When Jesus got in the boat, immediately the storm stopped and the boat was on the other side of Lake Galilee."

Ninepence frowned. Something didn't sound right . . . but she wasn't sure what it was. But the mule drivers didn't mind. They thought it was a great story.

The second night Yang told a story about Moses. "A great star appeared, and Moses led all the children of Israel to Bethlehem to see the Baby Jesus," he said happily.

The third night Yang said that Noah rescued the animals by sailing across the Red Sea, leaving the Egyptians to drown.

As Ninepence swung open the courtyard gate on the fourth evening, she wondered what kind of strange story Yang would tell tonight. Looking up and down the street for the mule trains, she saw a boy a few years older than she leaning against the wall outside the gate staring at her. He was barefoot and his once-blue jacket and trousers were dirty and torn. Ninepence didn't know whether to slam the gate shut or ask what he wanted, but before she could decide, the boy looked up at the *clop, clop, clop* of an approaching mule . . . and with a startled cry, he ran away.

Ninepence craned her neck to see if a mule train was coming . . . and saw instead a single mule and rider, flanked on either side by two soldiers.

"She's back!" she screamed, running inside and pulling on Yang's sleeve. "Come quickly . . . Gladys is back!"

There was hardly time for greetings and unpacking before the mule drivers started turning into the courtyard for the night. Yang generously offered to tell the Bible story to the mule drivers so that Gladys could eat her own supper. Gladys gratefully accepted and went upstairs to her room for some peace and quiet. But halfway through the story, she came downstairs to get another bowl of dough strings and vegetables and leaned against a doorpost, listening.

" . . . so Jesus spoke to Noah in a burning bush and said, 'You can eat the fruit of any tree in the garden except the Tree of Good and Evil.' But Noah's wife ate the forbidden fruit anyway, so God sent a big flood . . ."

"Oh dear," Gladys whispered to Ninepence, who was sitting on the floor, waiting to refill the cups of tea. "Has he been telling stories like this the whole time I was gone?"

The little girl nodded soberly. Gladys rolled her eyes and sighed . . . and then started to giggle. Now Ninepence knew her suspicion was correct: Yang had gotten the Bible stories all mixed up! Clamping a hand over her mouth, she tried to stifle her own giggles . . . but pretty soon the small Englishwoman and the little Chinese girl had to slip out to the courtyard, where they sat on the stone bench in the twilight and laughed and laughed.

The next day Gladys Aylward took Ninepence to the market in Yangcheng to buy wheat for making the noodlelike dough strings and a big bag of millet. They also bought a few carrots, turnips, tomatoes, and a cabbage from the farmers who grew vegetables in terraced fields on the mountainsides. Ninepence carried the vegetables tied on her back with a long strip of cloth, but Gladys carried the heavy bags of wheat and millet on the ends of a pole balanced across her shoulders, just like the Chinese women.

On their way back to the inn, Ninepence saw the same boy loitering outside the courtyard gate, but as soon as he saw them coming, he ran off.

All afternoon, Ninepence wondered why he had come twice to their gate. Curious, she finally tiptoed to the gate, opened it a crack, and peeked out. There was the boy staring back at her . . . and this time he was holding a small, empty bowl.

Ninepence quietly shut the gate and went back inside the inn, where Yang was dishing up the plain millet mush for their supper. They usually ate in the late afternoon before the mule trains arrived, when

everything got busy and hectic.

"Miss Gladys," Ninepence said shyly, looking at her bowl of steaming mush as they sat cross-legged on one of the brick *k'angs*, "if I took a little bit of my mush from my bowl, like this . . ." and Ninepence scooped some of her mush into an empty bowl, "what would I have in my bowl?"

Gladys Aylward looked at her curiously. "Why, you'd have a little less."

Ninepence pointed toward the courtyard. "There's a boy outside the gate with an empty bowl who has even less than my less. Could . . . could I give him my less, and then he'd have more than his less?"

Gladys' mouth twitched and she looked at Yang. "Why, uh . . . Yang, why don't you and I also put a spoonful of our mush into this bowl, and then we'd all have a little less, but the boy with less would have more?"

Yang smiled broadly, and soon the millet mush had been divided into four bowls instead of three. Without a word, Ninepence crawled off the *k'ang*, crossed the courtyard and opened the gate. The boy was still there. She opened the gate wider and beckoned him to come inside.

Urging the boy to follow, Ninepence led the way inside the inn. But once inside, the boy just stood there, holding his empty bowl and staring at Gladys, even when the Englishwoman held out the fourth bowl of mush.

"Here, give it to me," said Ninepence. She took the bowl of cooked millet and, with her chopsticks, scraped the mush into the boy's bowl. Immediately the boy sat down on the floor and hungrily scooped the warm food into his mouth.

"So," murmured Gladys, watching the boy eat, "this is 'Less,' the boy who has even less than our less."

The nickname stuck around . . . and so did the boy, whose story came out in bits and pieces. Bandits had raided his village up in the mountains. They had killed the men, burned the village, and taken the women and children with them. But the boy's mother had gotten sick on the forced march, and the bandits left her behind in a ditch to die. When the boy could not rouse his mother, he wandered from village to village begging food and had finally followed a mule train into Yangcheng.

The boy immediately attached himself to Ninepence, rarely letting her out of his sight. With a bath, a clean shirt and trousers, and a full belly, he looked like a new person. Soon the two children were chasing around the courtyard, playing tag, spreading fresh straw for the mules, and getting underfoot in the kitchen.

A few days later, Ninepence overheard Gladys and Yang talking in the kitchen. "Can we feed four mouths on our little income—especially a growing boy?" Gladys worried.

"Exactly!" Yang said. "A growing boy could be

very useful around here. You should not be mucking out that mule stable each day, Miss Gladys . . . and Yang's bones are too old for that kind of work."

"But . . . if he works for us, we should pay him," Gladys said in a worried voice.

"What do you mean, pay him?" scolded Yang. "Every son in a Chinese household has to do his chores!"

So Less stayed on at the Inn of Eight Happinesses, and it was just as Yang had said: a strong, young boy was very useful. Less took over the stable work, and the next time Gladys had to visit the mountain villages in her role as official Foot Inspector, Yang didn't have to hire any outside help, and they got along quite nicely . . . except that Yang still got his Bible stories mixed up.

When Gladys returned this time, she gathered Yang, Ninepence, and Less together and said, "While riding that bony old mule over the mountain passes, I had lots of time to think," she said. "Remember what you said, Yang, about how every son in a Chinese household has to do his chores?"

Yang nodded and smiled broadly. "Of course, of course. And Less has been very good about doing his chores."

Less ducked his head, embarrassed.

"Exactly!" agreed Gladys. "But . . . I've been thinking that we ought to make it official—about being a son, I mean."

The three Chinese faces stared back at her blankly. Whatever did she mean?

"What I mean is . . . I've been thinking . . . that is . . ." Gladys Aylward took a deep breath. "I would like to adopt Ninepence and Less as my very own children."

Now the three faces stared openmouthed.

"So . . . what do you think?" asked Gladys anxiously.

Ninepence found her voice first. "Would you be my mother then?"

"Yes . . . yes, I would," said Gladys, smiling.

"And would Ninepence be my sister?" said Less, his eyes wide.

Gladys nodded.

The children looked at each other, then at Yang, and back to Gladys. "Yes! Yes!" they shouted. "Hooray! Hooray!"

Gladys clapped her hands. *"How! How!* Good! Good!" she said. "Then we will go to the Mandarin tomorrow and make it official."

Chapter 5

Prison Riot!

NINEPENCE WAS NERVOUS. She had never been in the Mandarin's *yamen*—his official house—before. A servant in a blue brocade jacket and blue silk trousers opened the door and ushered them into a cool room. Decorated paper lanterns with tassles dangling from each corner hung along all the walls.

On tables of glossy, dark wood sat ancient porcelain bowls and vases. Sliding doors with elaborately painted scenes on paper panels led from one room to another.

Gladys had washed the

children's hair and scrubbed their clothes, but Ninepence still felt shabby in these elegant surroundings. "Never mind," Gladys whispered, reading her thoughts. "Just remember to bow respectfully to the Mandarin, and don't speak unless he speaks to you."

After waiting a few minutes, a paneled door slid open and the Mandarin stepped into the room. Ninepence and Less were so awed seeing the Mandarin that they almost forgot to bow. He was a tall man by Chinese standards, with high cheekbones and a mustache that hung below his jawline. Under his red silk cap, his hair formed a glossy, black pigtail that hung all the way down to his knees. He wore a long gown of red, blue, green, and gold; wide, embroidered sleeves hid his hands, which were grasped in front of him.

"Gladys Aylward, my friend," the Mandarin said warmly, crossing the room and dipping his head with pleasure toward the small Englishwoman. "What brings you to see me today? . . . And who are these children?"

Gladys bowed respectfully—though Ninepence noticed that she did not *kowtow* all the way to the floor as most people did when in the presence of the Mandarin. She put an arm around both Less and Ninepence. "These are orphan children I have taken into my home. I would like to adopt them as my own. Will you help me?"

The Mandarin arched an eyebrow. "Are you sure this is what you want to do—you, an Englishwoman?"

Gladys flushed. "Yes. China is my home now; your people are my people. These children have no one . . . except me."

"I see," said the Mandarin thoughtfully. "You have tried to locate their parents?"

Gladys told him what she knew of the children's background.

"Well, then," said the Mandarin, "there are papers which must be filled out . . ." He clapped his hands twice and a secretary appeared. Soon Gladys was seated at one of the glossy, wood tables, dipping a pen and writing on some official-looking papers.

The quietness of the room and the scratch, scratch, scratch of the pen were interrupted by a commotion outside the door. Angry voices rose, and then suddenly the door slid open and a very distraught man burst into the room.

"Governor!" exclaimed the Mandarin, frowning. "What is the meaning of this? Can't you see—"

"Excuse me, Excellency!" said the man, grabbing his cap off his head and *kowtowing* until his forehead touched the floor. Then he scrambled to his feet. "But this is a most extreme emergency! The prisoners—"

"One moment," the Mandarin interrupted, always aware of proper manners. "Miss Aylward, this is the Governor of the Prison. Honorable Governor, this is Miss Gladys Aylward, my official Foot Inspector."

The man kowtowed again, then blurted, "The prisoners are rioting! Oh! It is terrible! They are killing each other!"

"Why don't you send your soldiers in to stop it?"

demanded the Mandarin.

"These convicts are murderers, bandits, thieves!" protested the governor, twisting his cap in his hand. "There are not enough soldiers to stop the riot—they would almost certainly be killed! Come! Come quickly!"

Irritated, the Mandarin nonetheless clapped his hands, held a quick conference with his secretary, and was soon hurrying toward the prison with several guards and other officials. Not knowing what else to do, Gladys Aylward and the children hurried along with them.

As the little group turned down a narrow street, Ninepence could see the thick, stone walls of the prison at the other end. A great noise came from behind the walls—angry shouts, bloodcurdling yells, and screams of pain. Ninepence clung to Less's hand; she had seen the prison walls before but had never really thought about the people locked inside.

The Mandarin and the governor conferred briefly with the prison guards clustered anxiously outside the gate. Waves of invisible yells and screams from inside the wall made it almost impossible to talk or think. Ninepence saw that Gladys's eyes were closed and her lips moved, and the little girl knew that the missionary was praying. Then she realized everyone else was looking at Gladys, too.

The Mandarin broke away from the knot of officials and guards and approached Gladys. "Miss Aylward," he said, his face lined with deep concern, "you must go in and stop the riot."

"Me!" said Gladys, astonished. "I must go—! What are you talking about? Didn't you hear the governor say that the prisoners would kill the soldiers if they went in? If I went in, the prisoners would kill *me*!"

But the Mandarin was staring at Gladys with a strange look in his eyes. "No, no. How could they kill you? You tell our people that you have God living inside you . . ."

"G-God living inside . . . ?" stammered Gladys. "Well, yes, but—"

"I have heard about the stories you tell the mule drivers and the mountain people when you visit the villages as official Foot Inspector, have I not? Stories about God holding back a great sea and letting His people walk across on dry ground . . . about how God protected one of His prophets from being eaten by lions. If what you say is true, surely your God will protect you when you go inside the prison!"

The Mandarin spoke sincerely, his eyes pleading. Gladys was staring at him, openmouthed. Ninepence was so shocked she could hardly breathe; she knew that she was not supposed to speak unless spoken to in the presence of these important men . . . but inside she wanted to scream, "No! No! Don't send my mother in there! They will kill her!"

After what seemed like an eternity, Gladys Aylward swallowed and said quietly, "All right. Tell the governor to open the gate . . . I'll see what I can do. Less, hold tight to Ninepence; stay together no matter what happens."

Frightened, Less pulled Ninepence away from

the gate and held on to her with both hands. As Ninepence watched in horror, the big wooden gate was unbarred, swung open a crack, and the small Englishwoman in her plain blue shirt and trousers disappeared inside. Immediately the bar was dropped back in place.

Gladys Aylward was locked inside with a prison full of madmen!

Yang looked at Gladys in disbelief. "Why did you agree to such an insane idea! For a woman to go into a man's prison at any time is foolhardy . . . but in the middle of a riot—!"

Ninepence leaned against Gladys and looked up at her adopted mother's face. "Weren't you scared?" she said in a small voice.

Gladys Aylward took another comforting sip of hot, green tea. "Of course I was scared! But . . . I realized if I did not go in, I could forget about trying to be a missionary in China. I have been telling the people here that God is powerful, that He will protect them . . . but if I did not have enough faith to believe He would protect me . . ." Her voice trailed off.

"But what happened when the door was locked behind you?" Less asked anxiously. "For a while the screams and yells continued, and then all of a sudden it was quiet."

As they talked, Ninepence's thoughts wandered.

Was it only that morning they had gone to the *yamen* to meet the Mandarin and fill out the adoption papers? It seemed like years ago! Now they were sitting on one of the brick *k'angs* at the Inn of Eight Happinesses, drinking tea and trying to tell Yang what had happened. Even Ninepence and Less didn't know what happened . . . except that, after what seemed like hours, a knock was heard from the inside of the prison gate and Gladys came out again!

"Well," said Gladys, trying to fill them in, "when the gate locked behind me, I was terrified. I couldn't see anything at first because there was kind of a dark tunnel leading from the gate to the prison courtyard. But at the end of the tunnel, I could see men running this way and that, chasing one another with swords and knives, screaming like madmen. I'm not sure how I walked through the tunnel—my knees were shaking so badly—but suddenly I stepped out into the sunlight. Dead and wounded bodies were lying everywhere; the dirt was red with blood. I looked up . . . and there, running straight at me, was a giant of a man, holding an axe over his head."

A shiver of fear ran down Ninepence's spine, and goose bumps stood out all over her skin.

"I was so frightened I just stood there, as if my feet had been nailed into the ground," Gladys went on. "Suddenly the man stopped just a few feet away, holding his axe which was dripping with blood. Seeing me, one by one the other prisoners stopped chasing one another and walked slowly over to where I was standing."

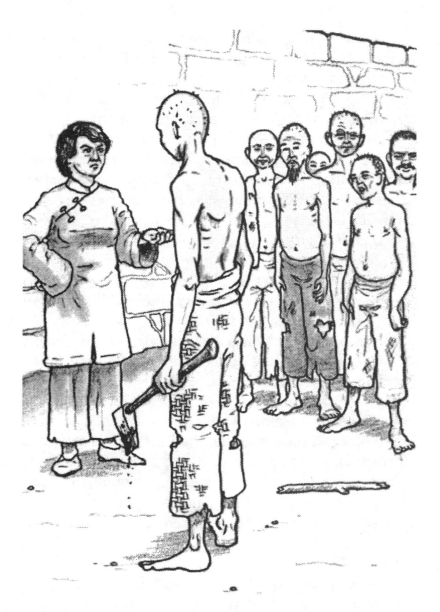

"Wh-what did you do?" asked Less, his eyes as big as teacups.

"I . . . well, I got mad! He was just a big bully, terrorizing the other prisoners with that axe. So I said very sternly, 'Give me that axe.' "

Yang blinked. "You said, 'Give me that axe'?!" The old man shook his head in amazement.

Gladys nodded. "And the man slowly handed me the axe. So . . . I gathered a little courage and said very boldly, 'All of you! Line up in front of me . . . two lines!' And all the men shuffled into two lines in front of me. But . . ." Gladys's voice broke, and she struggled to go on. "They were all so thin and bony. Their clothes were nothing more than dirty rags. I could see the hunger and misery in their eyes."

Ninepence pressed closer to Gladys. She remembered being hungry and dirty and cold . . . so miserable that she didn't care about anything anymore.

Gladys went on with her story. "I told them I was sent by the Governor of the Prison to find out why they were fighting. No one spoke, so I told them to appoint a spokesman. After a few moments, a young man stepped forward. I learned later that he was a former Buddhist priest who had been sentenced to eight years in prison for stealing money from the temple. 'My name is Feng,' he said politely. 'We are not sure how the fighting started. But . . . when men do not have enough to eat and nothing to do all day . . .' "

Gladys's eyes blazed. "Can you believe that, Yang? All those men locked up together, and no work to occupy their time. Of course they are going to get into fights! So I told Feng that if the men promised to be peaceful and clean up the courtyard and bury the dead, I would speak to the governor on their behalf."

"And she did!" Less crowed, laughing. "She gave that governor a talking to when she came out! She told him that he must find work for the men to do so they can earn money and buy food and have self-respect."

"Did he listen?" asked Yang.

"He better!" laughed Gladys. "Because I am going to visit Feng every day at the prison until it happens."

Suddenly Ninepence remembered something. "When it was all over," she told Yang, "we went back to the Mandarin's *yamen*—to finish the adoption papers, you know—and as we left, the Governor of the Prison said, 'Thank you, Ai-weh-deh.'"

"That's right," said Gladys thoughtfully. "Why do you think he called me Ai-weh-deh? Do you know what it means, Yang?"

A smile spread across Yang's round face. "'Ai-weh-deh'? Why, it means, 'The Virtuous One'!"

The story of Gladys Aylward stopping a riot in the Yangcheng prison spread quickly throughout the walled city and up and down the mule trails through the mountains. No one called the small English-woman who wore Chinese clothes a "foreign devil" anymore; in fact, no one called her Gladys Aylward anymore. Everywhere they went, Ninepence heard people say, "Good morning, Ai-weh-deh!" or "How about a nice cabbage today, Ai-weh-deh?" Even Yang used the new name when he fussed at her: "That coat is threadbare, Ai-weh-deh! You must have a new one before the snows come!"

Everyone except Less and Ninepence, that is. The night after the adoption papers were signed, Ninepence tugged shyly on Gladys's jacket sleeve. "Now that we are adopted," the six-year-old said anxiously, "can we—" She stopped, embarrassed.

"Can we call you Mama-san?" Less finished boldly.

"Of course!" Gladys said, gathering them both in a big bear hug. "You are my very own children now. Nothing and no one can take you away from me!"

Chapter 6

Breaking the Rules

AS THE WEATHER GOT COLDER and the first snows arrived in the mountains, fewer and fewer mule trains came through Yangcheng. Now Gladys and Yang and the children didn't have to work so hard running the Inn of Eight Happinesses . . . but on the other hand, it was hard work making food and other supplies stretch through the winter. Gladys cut up some of her old, wool English dresses and made new coats for the children to wear over their other old coats. And everyone

57

slept together on the brick *k'angs* at night to keep warm.

Ninepence, now seven years old, was glad when the snows finally began to melt and the spring sunshine brought back the birds and flowers in the mountain meadows. A few mule trains struggled up the rocky trail with welcome supplies of cloth, blankets, shoes, wheat, barley, millet, and vegetable seeds, bringing a few customers into the Inn of Eight Happinesses.

"What are they talking about?" Yang demanded of Less and Ninepence as the children hurried back and forth with cups of tea and bowls of millet mush for the hungry mule drivers.

"Oh . . . fighting down in the lowlands between the Chinese Communists and Nationalist soldiers," Less shrugged.

"Now, now," hushed Gladys, bustling into the kitchen, "let's not listen to rumors. Soldiers always find something to fight about. They won't bother us up here in the mountains. Why, we have enough to worry about with the local bandits!"

On the first really warm day, the women of Yangcheng gathered at the creek running down the mountainside near the East Gate to scrub their clothes on the rocks and catch up on all the gossip. Less and Ninepence helped Gladys lug all their winter clothes and bedding to the creek, and spent the morning dipping the clothes in the icy water, then pounding them on the rocks with a piece of wood.

"Do you know, Ai-weh-deh," said the woman next

to them, wringing creek water from her clothes as a baby snoozed on her back, "my husband followed one of the mule trains to Tsehchow to do some business, and he heard that Japanese soldiers have crossed the border into China."

"The Japanese?" another woman chimed in. "I have heard terrible things about those foreigners! Maybe we should move our families farther up the mountain."

"Hah!" said another eavesdropper. "Japan is no bigger than a toenail compared to our great country of China. Who's afraid of a toenail?"

"We mustn't act rashly," Gladys cautioned. "I traveled on a Japanese ship on the last leg of my journey to China, and the Japanese people were very kind and courteous. The Mandarin will let us know if there is any danger."

Ninepence was bored with this grown-up talk. She begged for permission to go play, and Gladys nodded absently.

For a while Ninepence and Less played tag with a few of the other children, jumping from rock to rock along the creek bank. Then she noticed a baby about two years old sitting alone on the rocks crying.

"Why is that little boy crying?" she asked anxiously, tugging on Less's coat sleeve.

"He must have lost his mama. Come on," said Less, scrambling over the rocks, "let's help him find her."

Ninepence wiped the baby's nose with her handkerchief; then Less picked him up and they started going from woman to woman along the creek bed, asking, "Do you know who this baby is? Do you know his mama?"

The women just shrugged or shook their heads. No one had ever seen this baby before.

"The mama's *got* to be here," said Less impatiently, putting down the little boy, who was very heavy even for a ten-year-old to carry. "This baby didn't just grow up out of the ground."

"Maybe he doesn't have a mama," Ninepence suggested.

"Of course he's got a mama!" said Less. "Come on, let's take him to Mama-san. She will know what to do." They each took one of the baby's hands, and he toddled between them as they slowly made their way back to Gladys, who was rolling their clean clothes into a wet bundle.

Gladys saw them coming. "What are you doing with that baby?" she called out. "Take him back to his mama, right this minute!"

"But that's the problem!" said Less. "We've been looking for his mama, but nobody has ever seen him before."

"Well . . . maybe he wandered away from the town. Somebody will come looking for him soon."

"But if nobody does, can he come home with us?" asked Ninepence hopefully.

"Absolutely not!" said Gladys, struggling up the bank with the heavy bundle of clothes. "We could be accused of child-stealing! Come on . . . we'll find his parents somehow."

But even though they asked everyone they met, no one had lost a baby. Gladys even went to see the Mandarin, who sent a town crier up and down the streets of Yangcheng announcing a lost child. Still no one claimed him.

Giving up, Gladys and the children finally took the little boy back to the Inn of Eight Happinesses. Ninepence begged some millet mush from Yang and spooned it into the baby's eager mouth, crooning softly, "This will fill your tummy, bao-bao . . ."

"I think this bao-bao has come to stay," Yang said, watching Ninepence feed the baby.

"Bao-Bao?" said Gladys frowning. "What does that mean?"

"Why, it means 'Precious Bundle,' " Yang grinned.

Ninepence came out of the stable, where she had been helping Less lay down fresh straw for the mules, and was surprised to see the Mandarin himself standing in their courtyard.

"But, Excellency," Gladys was protesting, bouncing Bao-Bao on her hip, "as you can see, my family has grown . . . and this one is just a baby. I cannot leave right now to visit the mountain villages."

The Mandarin tipped his head respectfully. "I understand, Ai-weh-deh. But the Nationalist government is getting very impatient to know whether their order to abolish foot-binding is being carried out in this region. And I have heard reports that a certain village is defying this order. You must go and enforce the law."

"But—"

"You are the only one who can do this, Ai-weh-deh," said the Mandarin firmly. "A woman must do this—a woman who does not have her feet bound. And now that you have also become a Chinese citizen, you speak not only with my authority but the authority of China!"

Ninepence poked Less and grinned. They had been so proud of their mama-san when she took the oath of citizenship—the same day she signed papers to adopt Bao-Bao.

"But—"

"I will provide another mule for you," the Mandarin went on. "You can take your little one with you, and"—he nodded toward Ninepence—"a mother's helper." Then he looked down at Ninepence's feet. "Besides, this young lady's unbound feet will be a good example."

There was not much use protesting. An order was an order. Ninepence felt very grown up riding on the big mule a few days later as it lurched and swayed up the rocky mule track. Gladys and Bao-Bao were riding on the mule in front of her, accompanied by three foot soldiers to lead the mules and protect the little caravan from bandits. Yang and Less had been left behind to take care of the mule drivers stopping at the Inn of Eight Happinesses.

When they rode into the high mountain village in late afternoon, Gladys went right to work, calling

the villagers together, reading the Mandarin's order, and asking to see all young girls under the age of twelve. The mothers and fathers were sullen but grudgingly cooperated when the soldiers made it clear that they had no choice. Gladys showed them how to *slowly* unbind their little girls' tortured feet, bathing and massaging the little misshaped toes. Ninepence played with Bao-Bao so Gladys could work . . . but she proudly showed off her strong, straight feet when Gladys asked her to walk back and forth in front of the villagers.

As twilight settled over the mountains, Gladys went from house to house, knocking on each door, to make sure that no little girls had been missed. At one house, a sturdy mountain woman just glared at them and would not let them in.

"My master is not at home. I cannot let you in," she said stubbornly. "He gave me firm orders. He—"

"What is your name, Mrs.—?" asked Gladys pleasantly.

"Mrs. Cheng. I am housekeeper here. You may not come in."

"Well, Mrs. Cheng," said Gladys, "I have orders from the Mandarin—"

But before she could politely persuade the woman to let them in, the soldiers simply shoved the woman aside and barged in.

"Get out! Get out!" yelled the woman. "You have no right—!"

"Mama-san . . . look!" said Ninepence, holding Bao-Bao tightly on her hip with one hand and pointing with the other.

There, on a straw mat in a corner of the room, lay a small girl about four years old, whimpering and sucking her thumb, her tiny feet bound in the traditional manner.

"All right, all right . . . there is one girl child," Mrs. Cheng admitted reluctantly. "But she is not mine . . . she belongs to my master! He will be very angry if I let you unbind her feet!"

"Still . . . it must be done," said Gladys, kneeling down beside the girl and starting the slow process of unwrapping her poor, painful feet. "It is the law."

Instead of squirming fearfully, as most little girls did when Gladys tried to unwrap their feet, this one submitted meekly and even smiled at Ninepence.

"What is your name?" Gladys asked gently as she unwrapped the second foot and began massaging the bent toes.

"Tiger Lily," the little girl whispered.

"Do not talk to strangers!" yelled Mrs. Cheng, who was pacing angrily up and down the room. "You know the rules!"

But Tiger Lily looked at Gladys, Ninepence, and Bao-Bao with eager eyes. "Are you going to unwrap the feet of Precious Pearl, too? And Jade Lily . . . and Glorious Ruby . . . and Crystal?" she asked shyly.

"What?" said Gladys in astonishment. She whirled on Mrs. Cheng. "There are other children here! Where are they, you evil woman? Tell me now, or it is prison for you!"

Again, the soldiers did not wait. They searched

the house and found four other little girls—all about the same age as Tiger Lily—locked in a back room.

Ninepence was confused. How could one family have so many girls the same age? But Gladys was not confused; she was furious.

"Your master is not the father of these girls!" she shouted at Mrs. Cheng. "Who are they? Why are they here?"

Frightened, Mrs. Cheng admitted that her master had bought all five girls from families who did not want them, and he was going to sell them for a good price when their feet were "ready" and he found either husbands or brothels willing to pay for them.

Now it was Gladys Aylward who was angrily pacing up and down the room. The five little girls sat mute and frightened in the corner. Bao-Bao began to cry.

Gladys stopped pacing. "We will spend the night here," she announced. "Tomorrow morning at first light, I am taking all five girls with me to Yangcheng. If we leave them here, their feet will be re-bound, and they will be sold like slaves. I will not let it happen! That is my decision."

A strange procession the next morning started down the mountain trail from the village. First came a soldier leading Gladys Aylward's mule, carrying Gladys, Bao-Bao, Precious Pearl, and Glorious Ruby. Next came the second soldier leading the second mule, carrying Ninepence, Tiger Lily, Jade Lily, and Crystal. At the rear walked the third soldier, rifle ready, keeping a watch for bandits.

But no sooner had they lost sight of the village than someone came running down the trail after them, shouting, "Wait! Wait!" Ninepence twisted around on the mule and saw the lone figure of a woman shuffling toward them on her small feet. The soldiers shrugged and didn't stop, but by sliding down the side of the trail and catching them as the trail bent around a curve, the woman soon caught up to them.

It was Mrs. Cheng.

"Ai-weh-deh! Ai-weh-deh!" she cried, tugging on Gladys's trousers. "Take me with you! If my master returns and finds the girls gone, he will beat me . . . or even kill me! Please take me with you!"

Gladys looked at the girls and then at the soldiers. No one said anything or made any movement that hinted yes or no.

Gladys sighed. "All right," she agreed. "But . . . I'm sorry, Mrs. Cheng. The mules are loaded. You will have to walk to Yangcheng."

Chapter 7

Stranger in the Street

NINEPENCE WAS EXCITED: overnight she had become a "big sister" to five little girls who followed her around the Inn of Eight Happinesses like little chicks. At first she didn't notice that Less seemed sullen at the appearance of Mrs. Cheng and the flock of four- and five-year-olds. But when he disappeared for several hours on the second day, Ninepence went looking for him.

She found Less sulking in the stable. "What's the matter?" she asked anxiously. "Aren't you happy that Tiger Lily and the other girls are safe now with Ai-weh-deh?"

Less scuffed the straw with his foot. "Well, yes, I guess, but . . ." The boy looked uncomfortable. "But . . . now you have many playmates, and I will have no one . . . except Bao-Bao, and he's just a baby."

Ninepence slipped her hand into his reassuringly. "Don't be sad," she said. "You are my very own adopted brother—you and Bao-Bao. You will always be my very best friend."

Less looked at her doubtfully. "Truly?"

"Truly! Now, come on," she said, tugging on his sleeve, "we can both help Mama-san by rubbing the little girls' feet and helping them get straight and strong—like mine!"

With eight children running around the court-yard that year, life at the Inn of Eight Happinesses was loud and lively, full of little joys and problems—squealing games of tag and leapfrog . . . constant runny noses . . . washing and mending endless pairs of blue jackets and trousers . . . scoldings from Yang for not emptying the slop bucket or forgetting to put away the bowls and teacups . . . climbing the mountainside for a summer picnic . . . listening wide-eyed as Gladys told endless bedtime Bible stories . . . then eavesdropping at the cracks in the second floor (when the children were supposed to be asleep) as Gladys told the Bible stories all over again to the mule drivers.

Mrs. Cheng stayed for a few weeks, but she was afraid her old master would find her and beat her, and one day she just disappeared. Tiger Lily whispered to Ninepence that she was glad Mrs. Cheng was gone. "She used to beat us, too," the little girl confided. "The only reason she didn't dare hit us here is because she was afraid of Ai-weh-deh."

"Afraid?" said Ninepence, wondering how anyone could be afraid of her gentle Mama-san, who was only five feet tall.

"Oh, yes," said Tiger Lily solemnly. "Everybody up the mountain knows that Ai-weh-deh defeated a hundred axe-murderers with one hand tied behind her back."

When Ninepence told Less what Tiger Lily had said, they laughed and laughed—and decided to keep it a secret. If Ai-weh-deh knew what people were saying, she would make it her business to set the record straight . . . but Ninepence and Less thought this rumor might make bandits leave Ai-weh-deh alone when she had to visit the mountain villages in her role as official Foot Inspector.

As the two oldest of the eight children, Ninepence and Less were often sent on errands to the market or with messages. As spring turned to summer, and summer to fall, they noticed more Nationalist army officers coming through Yangcheng on their big, strong horses; sometimes two or three of them would even stay at the Inn of Eight Happinesses. But usually they had official business with the Mandarin and other city officials, or were on their way over the mountains to Sian in the next province, and in a few days they moved on again.

One day in late fall, Gladys came home from a visit to the Mandarin looking a little flushed and distracted. "I met a very interesting army officer today at the *yamen*," she told Yang and the children as they ate their supper of dough strings, chicken, and vegetables. "His name is Colonel Linnan—he's an intelligence officer, I think, for General Chiang Kai-shek's Nationalist army. Strange . . . he's a very cultured young man, schooled in philosophy, speaks classical Mandarin Chinese . . . we had a very interesting conversation! Too bad he ended up in the army."

But Gladys had too much on her mind to pay much attention to interesting army officers. The winter of 1935 and '36 was, as Yang described it, a "three-coat winter," burying Yangcheng under snow for months at a time. The bitter cold seeped through the drafty old inn, and at night they all huddled on the warm, brick *k'angs*—grateful, at least, that the deep snow meant no mule drivers came to stay at the inn.

But Ninepence and Less knew that Gladys and Yang worried about whether their supply of coal and food would last the winter. Vegetables, eggs, and the occasional chicken were soon memories, and by January, Yang was serving bread, potatoes, and millet mush for both breakfast and supper. Still, Gladys taught the children a "thank-you song" to sing each meal before they ate their meager food:

Count your blessings,
Name them one by one.
Count your blessings,
See what God has done.
Count your blessings!
Name them one by one!
Count your many blessings,
See what God has done.

When the snow finally began to thaw, the children gleefully pranced in the puddles in the courtyard.

"Look! Look!" squealed Glorious Ruby. "I see a red bird—there! On the courtyard wall!"

"I saw it first . . . didn't I see it first, Ninepence?" wailed Precious Pearl.

"Crystal! Jade Lily! Put on your coats!" scolded Less, who was now eleven and took his "big brother" role very seriously.

"Ah, the sweet sounds of spring," joked Yang from the doorway as Ai-weh-deh, watching the eight children get sopping wet in the slushy snow, rolled her eyes helplessly.

Then one day, as the snow continued melting, Less really did have news. "Mama-san! Ninepence! Yang! Come quickly. A mule train is coming over the mountain!"

Ai-weh-deh and the children all ran out into the

courtyard and looked where Less was pointing—not down toward the valley, where the first mule trains were usually spotted coming from Tsehchow, but at the high, rocky trails coming from the other side of the mountains and the Yellow River valley. A long line of black dots seemed to creep down the mountainside. But there was something strange about this mule train . . .

As the black dots grew larger, the citizens of Yangcheng realized this wasn't a mule train at all. Men, women, and children—lots of children—carrying bundles on their backs straggled wearily into the city streets. Less was sent to find out what was happening and returned with grim news.

"The Yellow River has flooded from the spring thaw!" he reported. "All these people have lost their farms and villages, and . . . a lot of people have drowned, too."

Just then there was a banging at the courtyard gate. Ai-weh-deh looked at Yang. Ninepence knew what her adopted mother was thinking. All these refugees needed a place to stay . . . but how could they feed more mouths when the mule trains hadn't yet arrived from Tsehchow, bringing new supplies? But with a deep breath, Ai-weh-deh went to the courtyard gate and threw it open.

"*Lai-lai-lai!*" she called. "Come, come, come! You can sleep here. Lots of room . . . *Lai-lai-lai!*"

All the inns of Yangcheng were full that night, and many citizens took refugees into their homes as well. Within a few days, many of the refugees had

moved on to live with relatives in other towns and villages; some built temporary huts outside the city walls until they could find proper work and housing. The Mandarin held emergency meetings with city officials to discuss the problem of feeding the remaining refugees . . . and the ones still coming over the mountain. But even when rations of wheat and barley and millet had been shared with the newcomers, there was still another problem: what to do with the children who had lost their parents in the flood.

The Mandarin sent a messenger asking Ai-weh-deh to come to the *yamen*. When she returned, she sat down wearily and looked around at her brood of eight: three adopted children and five orphans. Bao-Bao climbed in her lap and stuck his thumb in his mouth.

"Well?" asked Yang, hands on his hips.

Ai-weh-deh sighed. "There are sixteen children at the *yamen* . . . orphans of the Yellow River flood. The Mandarin asked me . . ." Her voice trailed off.

There was silence as the children looked at one another. Then five-year-old Crystal—the youngest of the five orphans—said shyly, "Ai-weh-deh, I will eat a little less . . ."

"Me too!" piped up first one and then another.

Less nodded. "We will all share . . . just like the boy in the Bible who gave his lunch to Jesus!"

"After all, Mama-san," Ninepence giggled, "sixteen is not so many . . . much less than the five thousand people that Jesus fed with one lunch."

Ai-weh-deh threw up her hands. "How can you argue with the faith of children?" she laughed ruefully.

So it was decided. Soon the Inn of Eight Happinesses rang with the shouts, quarrels, laughter, and tears of twenty-four children ranging in age from two to fifteen. The Mandarin squeezed some money out of the *yamen* treasury to help support the orphans; some of the farmers around Yangcheng "just happened" to leave a bag of wheat or a bucket of fresh eggs at the gate; and as the mule trains started their treks over the mountains with food and supplies to sell, sometimes the mule drivers who stayed at the inn "forgot" a bolt of cloth or some warm blankets and left them behind.

"See how God knows what we need?" Ai-weh-deh marveled to the children one day as Yang came home from the market with yet another basket of wilted vegetables a vendor had put aside for "Ai-weh-deh's orphans." "Now we must pray for a school—there's no way I can teach all of you to read and write Chinese by myself!"

Ninepence trudged through the streets of Yangcheng toward the prison, carrying five-year-old Bao-Bao on her back. It had been almost two years since the Governor of the Prison had offered to help Ai-weh-deh start a school for her orphans. "I have three children," he explained to Ai-weh-deh, "and there are other parents in Yangcheng who want their children to have more schooling than they can give them at home. If all the parents pay something, we can hire a teacher!"

Rumors of advancing Japanese soldiers became

more frequent, as well as reports of fighting between the Chinese Nationalist and Communist soldiers in some of the other provinces. In fact, once a whole company of Chinese Communist soldiers marched into Yangcheng. Everyone stared and wondered at the sudden disappearance of the Nationalist soldiers who had become commonplace by then. But after three days, the Communist soldiers marched on, and life in Yangcheng went on as usual in spite of the interruption.

It was now spring again, 1938; Ninepence was ten years old and Less was thirteen. Some of the Yellow River flood orphans had been located by frantic relatives and taken to live with uncles and aunts or grandparents . . . but somehow, other ragged boys or unwanted girls found their way to the Inn of Eight Happinesses to fill their place, so there were still about twenty-five children—more or less—who trekked from the inn to the governor's school near the prison.

One day Ninepence felt a strange dread as the noisy group of children drew closer to the old guardhouse the Governor of the Prison had remodeled into a school building. Two days in a row she had seen a strange man standing in the street when she came out of school, and he had seemed to be looking right at her. She hadn't told anyone . . . what was there to tell? Nothing had happened. Maybe she had just imagined that he was staring at her.

Still, it felt comforting to carry Bao-Bao on her back. At five, her little brother was big enough to walk to school by himself, but when she offered him a piggyback ride, he crowed with delight. As she turned the last corner, she tightened her grip on Bao-Bao's legs . . . then felt a great sigh of relief when she saw that the stranger wasn't there.

How silly she had been! she chided herself as Bao-Bao slid to the ground. "Wait for me after school right here!" she called after him as he went running into the courtyard with the younger children.

Bao-Bao was waiting at the gate as she came out after school. "Come on . . . come on!" he whined, pulling at her hand. "I wanna go home and get something to eat."

"Wait just a minute, Bao-Bao," Ninepence said. "Less isn't here yet . . . I want to wait for him and Tiger Lily."

Bao-Bao plopped down in the dusty street. Ninepence leaned against the gate and watched idly as the little boy picked up pebbles and threw them against the wall surrounding the school. She wished Less would hurry up. Lessons had been hard . . . who cared about the Ming Dynasty, which ruled China hundreds of years ago? She wanted to go home, too.

Just then she felt someone grab her by the arm. "Oh, good," she said, "there you are, Less . . ."

She looked up—right into the face of the strange man.

Chapter 8

Out of the Past

L ET GO OF ME!" NINEPENCE CRIED, jerking her arm away.

"Don't be scared, Mei-en," said the man, grinning. He was missing several teeth. "I just want to talk to you."

Ninepence was frightened. No one had called her Mei-en since . . . since she'd come to live with Ai-weh-deh. How did this strange man know her other name? Her instinct was to run . . . but she couldn't just leave Bao-Bao.

"I don't want to talk to you!" she said crossly, and hauled Bao-Bao to his feet by the back of his collar.

Just then Less pushed his way between Ninepence and the strange man. "What do you want?" he demanded. "Leave my sister alone!"

"Your *sister*?" laughed the man. "That's what you think. Be quiet, boy—I just want to talk to Mei-en."

"Ninepence . . . Bao-Bao . . . we're going home right now!" ordered Less, taking both of them by the hand and pulling them down the street.

Ninepence's heart was thumping wildly. Less was walking fast, practically lifting a wailing Bao-Bao off his feet. Was the man following them? At the corner, she sneaked a look over her shoulder. The man was still standing by the school gate, watching them with a sour look on his face.

When the children burst into the door of the Inn of Eight Happinesses, they saw that Ai-weh-deh was having tea with Colonel Linnan, the handsome Nationalist army in- telligence officer who often came to visit. Seeing their stricken faces, Ai- weh-deh immedi-  ately said, "Less—Ninepence—what's the matter? Is it one of the children—?"

The story came out all in a rush, with Less and Ninepence both talking at the same time and Bao- Bao pulling on Ai-weh-deh's sleeve, whining, "I'm hungry, Mama-san."

Tiger Lily and the other children soon came in noisily and were hurried away by Yang to do their chores; Bao-Bao was finally pacified with a handful of peanuts from Colonel Linnan as Less added indignantly, "That man called Ninepence *Mei-en*, Mama-san. Why did he call her that?"

"Well," said Ai-weh-deh slowly, her arm around Ninepence, "Mei-en is her real name . . . it's on her adoption papers, just like your real name—Sheng-Li—is on your adoption papers, Less. But . . . but . . . ." Ai-weh-deh flashed a worried look at Colonel Linnan. "Could it be someone who knew Ninepence before . . . before I found her?"

"*Mei-en* . . . 'Beautiful Grace,' " the colonel murmured. "This man . . . had you ever seen him before, Ninepence?"

Ninepence shook her head tearfully. "Only two days ago, I saw him standing outside the school. He was looking at me."

Ai-weh-deh was upset. "Colonel," she said, "can't we have this man arrested? Now . . . before something worse happens?"

Colonel Linnan shook his head thoughtfully. "All we have is the word of the children. This man must be caught in the act before he can be arrested."

"Caught in the act?" cried Ai-weh-deh. "But . . . how—?"

"Well, now," said Colonel Linnan calmly, "I think I have a plan . . ."

Ninepence's knees shook as she, Less, and the other children from the Inn of Eight Happinesses approached the school the next morning. Glancing out of the corner of her eye, she saw a man walking slowly alongside them, a wide straw hat hiding his face in shadow, his shoulders bent under a long pole on which hung two heavy market baskets.

Only she and Less and Ai-weh-deh knew it was Colonel Linnan in disguise.

Ninepence looked fearfully about, but the strange man was nowhere to be seen. She hurried into the school but could not concentrate on her studies. When the teacher called on her, asking what country invaded China in 1644 and overthrew the Ming Dynasty, Ninepence only stared stupidly at her feet.

Finally the long school day was over. Again, Ninepence's knees shook as she came outside. She tried to remember what Colonel Linnan had told her . . . she must stand by the gate, as if waiting for the other children to come outside, giving the strange man a chance to approach her once more.

But Ninepence was afraid. She couldn't see the man with the straw hat and long pole . . . what if the strange man came and Colonel Linnan wasn't there to help her?

More and more children spilled out of the school. Ninepence was jostled at the gate as the children, laughing and calling to each other, ran into the street. Ninepence's school books were accidently knocked out of her hands and she stooped to pick them up.

The next thing she knew, she was being jerked to her feet and pulled along by the strange man. Panicking, she screamed, "Let me go! Let me go!"

Suddenly, another yell cut the air. Seemingly from out of nowhere, Less threw himself at the strange man, beating on him with his fists and kicking with his feet. "Let go of her!" shouted Less, grabbing the man's hair and holding on tight.

But the man's iron grip on Ninepence's arm tightened. He shook Less off and pulled Ninepence, screaming, down the street. In a split second Less was back again, and this time he bit down—hard—on the man's arm.

With a yelp of pain, the man let go of Ninepence. "Run!" yelled Less and pulled Ninepence away.

At that same moment Ninepence saw the man in the straw hat appear and she heard Colonel Linnan's voice shouting sternly, "Don't move! You are under arrest!"

The next day a messenger came to the Inn of Eight Happinesses asking for Ai-weh-deh and Ninepence to come to the *yamen* to see the Mandarin.

Ninepence clung tightly to Ai-weh-deh's hand as a servant ushered them into the Mandarin's receiving room. Colonel Linnan was there, dressed once more in his army uniform, and the strange man leaned indolently against a table, a sour look on his face. He glared at Ninepence for a brief moment as she came in, then turned his head and ignored her.

Ninepence heard a sliding door open, and the

Mandarin stepped into the room, wearing his long, flowing robe of rich colors, his folded hands hidden as always in the wide sleeves. The stranger immediately *kowtowed* to the floor; Colonel Linnan bowed respectfully from the waist; Ai-weh-deh and Ninepence politely bowed their heads.

"Sit down, all of you," the Mandarin invited politely. When everyone was seated, he continued. "I called you here, Ai-weh-deh, because I think you need to hear what this man has to say. Now, sir," he turned to the stranger, "tell us who you are."

The man cleared his throat. "My name is Wang-Lu Chou. I am the only living son of Mrs. Mei-Ling Chou." The man darted a glance at Ninepence.

"Go on," prompted the Mandarin.

"My mother, Mrs. Chou, had another son, Yung-Wu, who was killed eight years ago in an accident on the mountain. This girl . . ."—the man jerked his head at Ninepence—"Mei-en Chou . . . is my brother's child. I am her uncle."

Ninepence felt as if the breath had been knocked out of her. Her uncle! Her father's own brother! But . . . why had he tried to frighten her? Why had he tried to steal her away?

"But . . . how did you know she was here in Yangcheng?" cried Ai-weh-deh.

The man shrugged. "Word gets around. My mother knew the girl was living with the foreign devil."

"She *knew*?" gasped Ai-weh-deh. Ninepence saw the color creep up her adopted mother's neck and knew she was getting angry. "Did this Mrs. Chou also know that I have adopted her? Ninepence . . . Mei-en . . . is my daughter now."

The man shrugged again, as if he didn't care. But Ai-weh-deh wasn't through. "Then why have you come to see the child now, after so many years?" she demanded. "Her grandmother didn't want her . . . she sold her to a gypsy, like so much trash. The child was nearly dead when I . . . found her."

"*Bought* her, you mean," the man sneered.

"B—but . . . I—I . . ." Ai-weh-deh stammered.

"Come, come," interrupted Colonel Linnan. "Let us get to the point. The fact is that this man was arrested—*I* arrested him—for trying to kidnap the child. Now it turns out he is related to her. Speak up, man—what is your business with the girl?"

Wang-Lu smiled smugly. "I only wanted to talk to the girl . . . but she made it so difficult. You see, my mother, Mrs. Chou, recently died, and I am her only living relative . . . along with my brother's child, of course," he added hastily. "There is the matter of the inheritance, you see."

"Oh, yes, I see," said Ai-weh-deh sarcastically. "I suppose you are very concerned that Ninepence— Mei-en—gets her share."

"Well," Wang-Lu said, tipping his head politely toward the Mandarin, "as His Excellency knows, Chinese law says that all inheritance money and property must be divided equally among the heirs. However, it would be a shame if the family farm had to be sold and divided up . . . so I thought, if Mei-en came to live with me, I could manage her share, and when I died, she would, of course, inherit from me."

A stab of fear went through Ninepence. Go to live with this . . . this stranger? She turned pleading eyes on Ai-weh-deh. Ai-weh-deh squeezed her hand reassuringly and turned to the Mandarin.

"Your Excellency," she pleaded, "you cannot let this man lay claim to Ninepence. The Chous obviously didn't want her . . . until now. But now she is my adopted daughter!"

"And I am her blood uncle!" interrupted Wang-Lu angrily. "Which do you think will hold up in a court of law?"

The Mandarin held up his hand. "The man does have a case, Ai-weh-deh, which must be settled in court."

"In court?"

The Mandarin nodded. He looked at Ai-weh-deh and a small smile played on his lips, but all he said was, "All must be done properly and in order."

The court hearing dragged on for two weeks. Colonel Linnan had to go back to Tsehchow on pressing army business, but Ai-weh-deh and Ninepence went to the courtroom every day.

Wang-Lu Chou's lawyer argued hotly that Mei-en Chou should be returned to her natural family— meaning her uncle—and keep the Chou family and its inheritance together. Weren't blood relations more important than a so-called "mother" who simply "bought" a child? Not only that, the lawyer pointed out, the woman called Ai-weh-deh was really Gladys Aylward, an *Englishwoman* by birth, and since Mei-en was a minor, did the court want a *foreigner* handling the inheritance of a Chinese family?

The court-appointed lawyer representing Ninepence argued that the uncle *had* tried to kidnap the girl, and no telling what would have happened to her if he had succeeded! Had Wang-Lu Chou or the grandmother shown any interest in the girl prior to this? If the girl was out of the way, then the uncle would be the sole inheritor. And the court should remember, the lawyer argued, if Ai-weh-deh had not rescued Mei-en Chou—also known as Ninepence— she would probably not be alive today.

Finally the Mandarin was ready to give his decision. Ninepence was so nervous she couldn't eat her breakfast that morning. She tried not to think what would happen if the Mandarin said she had to go live with her uncle! "Trust God," Ai-weh-deh whispered to her as they served tea and millet mush sweetened with sorghum to the mule drivers who had spent the night in the inn. *Trust God*, she thought as she helped the younger children get ready for school.

At the last minute, Bao-Bao ran back and gave Ninepence a hug. Then, blinking back anxious tears, Ninepence walked hand in hand with Ai-weh-deh to the Mandarin's court.

Chapter 9

Fire From the Sky

A SLEEPY-LOOKING CLERK droned, "Case 685, Wang-Lu Chou versus Mei-en Chou . . . the court has reached a verdict. All stand."

Ai-weh-deh and Nine-pence stood facing the Mandarin alongside Wang-Lu Chou, who was looking sour as usual. Ninepence's mouth was so dry she could hardly swallow.

The Mandarin stood, regal and impassive, as he read his verdict. "This court recognizes Gladys Aylward, known as Ai-weh-deh, 'The Virtuous One,' as the legal guardian of Mei-en Chou, ten years old, also known as Ninepence."

Ninepence started to squeal with excitement, but a sober frown from the Mandarin silenced her. "The inheritance of Mrs. Mei-Ling Chou consists of both land and money," he continued, "which the court determines to be about equal in value. Ai-weh-deh, as Mei-en's legal guardian, you may choose which half you desire: land or money. The other half will suffice as the inheritance for Wang-Lu Chou."

Ai-weh-deh stared in amazement at the Mandarin. "*I* should choose?" she asked. The small English-woman looked at Ninepence, who at ten years of age stood only a few inches shorter than she. "What use is land to us at the Inn of Eight Happinesses? We cannot farm it. But money . . . that can be saved for Ninepence's education and a dowry when she gets married." Ai-weh-deh turned back to the Mandarin. "We choose the money."

Wang-Lu Chou tilted his chin up. "The farm is mine?" His sour face actually cracked a smile. "It is a good decision. *How-how!* Good! Good!" And without a backward glance, the man hurried from the court-room and was gone.

When the other children arrived home from school, they clamored around Ninepence, wanting to know what happened.

"Is that evil man gone?" Less demanded.

When Ai-weh-deh smiled and said, "Gone for good!" the boy seemed to relax for the first time in weeks.

After the story had been told at least twice, Ai-weh-deh clapped her hands and said, "Now go . . . go! Do your chores. The mule trains will be coming into the city any time now and we must be ready."

Less and two of the older boys hurried out to the stable to clean out the old straw and lay down fresh. Ninepence and some of the older girls were assigned to chop vegetables in the kitchen, while Tiger Lily, Glorious Ruby, and Jade Lily played games with Bao-Bao and the other little ones in the courtyard.

Soon the courtyard gates were opened wide, and the first mule train clopped into the stone courtyard. The head mule driver was Hsi-Lien, one of their regulars. He was also the first mule driver to become a Christian. Usually, Hsi-Lien teased the children and ended up giving piggyback rides around the courtyard—even after a long day on the mountain trail! But today Hsi-Lien wore a long face and didn't seem to notice the children.

"Whatever is troubling you, my friend?" asked Ai-weh-deh as Less and several boys helped the mule drivers pull the heavy packs off the weary mules.

Hsi-Lien shook his head. "The news . . . it is very bad. When we stopped in Luan several days ago, the people were worried about a Japanese attack."

"Luan!" exclaimed Ai-weh-deh. "But that's in our very own province! Surely the Japanese haven't advanced this far!"

"Oh, but they have," said Hsi-Lien. "They have already pushed across the border of northern Shansi! How many days will it take for them to come this far south? My wife, my children . . . they are alone in my village."

"Well, well," said Ai-weh-deh thoughtfully. "Remember we are up in the mountains along a mule track! There is no road for army trucks. But, when you are worried, it is important to pray. Come on . . . we will go pray now, before supper!"

A few other Christians in Yangcheng, hearing the ominous news from other mule trains coming into the city, hurried to the inn, and the impromptu prayer meeting moved to the second floor. Yang shook his head and complained about his supper getting cold, but he, too, joined the small prayer meeting. Ninepence and the other children ran out into the courtyard, enjoying their extra playtime, as the other mule drivers rubbed down their animals in the stable.

"Look, Ninepence, look!" cried Bao-Bao, pointing at the sky. "Pretty birds!"

Ninepence shielded her eyes against the late afternoon sun sinking toward the mountains in the west and looked north toward Tsehchow. Three silver birds flew out of the clouds.

The other small children shouted and clapped their hands. "Oh, look!" . . . "Pretty, pretty!"

Less shielded his eyes and squinted. "I don't think those are birds," he said. "They are airplanes!"

"Airplanes! Airplanes!" the children squealed.

None of them had ever seen an airplane before, but they had heard about the "metal birds."

By now, the street outside the Inn of Eight Happinesses was filling up as men, women, and children came out of their homes to see the unusual sight. Ninepence could hear a sound now, growing louder and louder as the airplanes circled to the left and flew lower and lower.

"Look, look!" cried Bao-Bao, pointing again. "The silver birds are dropping something! Maybe they are sending us presents!" The five-year-old giggled. This was exciting!

Goose bumps crawled down Ninepence's arms as she watched the strange objects falling from the sky. Whatever could they be? What if they fell on someone and hurt—?

At that moment, a big explosion somewhere in the city sent fire, wood, and rocks hurtling into the sky. Then another explosion . . . and another! The children's laughter turned to screams and panic as they rushed to get inside the inn. The planes roared overhead, circled around the valley, and started to fly low over Yangcheng again.

"Mama-san!" screamed Ninepence, still standing in the courtyard. She had seen the rising sun painted on the airplane wings. "Japanese!" she screamed again.

Less ran back out into the courtyard and grabbed Ninepence by the arm. "Get inside!" he yelled.

Just then Ninepence heard a loud whistling sound . . . and suddenly an explosion knocked the two children to the ground. The air filled with fire, smoke, and flying debris. Less threw his body over Ninepence's, pressing her face against the rough cobblestones as pieces of wood and stone rained down on them.

And then . . . silence. Stunned, Less and Ninepence sat up and looked around them. A corner of the Inn of Eight Happinesses had been blown away. The second-floor balcony hung at a rakish angle. Ninepence heard the mules begin braying frantically from the stable . . . but other than that, there was a strange silence.

And then the wailing started. Beyond the court-yard, out in the streets, people wailing. Then . . . a new sound, closer—the whimpers and cries of chil-dren from inside the inn.

Ninepence scrambled to her feet. Her face stung where it had been pressed into the cobblestones, but she had no broken bones. Without even thinking, she ran to the door, which was hanging open, and dashed inside.

It took several seconds for her eyes to adjust to the half-light. Several of the beams holding up the second floor had collapsed, and half the ceiling was hanging down, almost touching the floor. Ninepence glanced around frantically. On the side of the room where the ceiling was still up, she saw a frightened knot of children huddled in a corner, crying.

Bao-Bao saw her and held up his arms, his whim-pers turning to loud wails of relief. Ninepence picked him up, heavy as he was, and hugged him tightly, realizing he was all right. All the other children seemed basically unhurt as well, except for scratches and bruises.

Then she heard Less calling her from the other side of the big room. "Ninepence! Go get help! I think Mama-san and Yang and the others are buried underneath these beams!"

Dumping Bao-Bao with Tiger Lily, Ninepence ran outside—right into the dazed mule drivers who were just now venturing out of the stable to see what had happened. Quickly the men went to work, pulling aside large pieces of the ceiling, lifting the big wooden beams.

A moan drifted out from the debris. "She's here! She's here!" screamed Less, frantically digging through the wood and plaster. Ai-weh-deh was lying face down on the floor, a large beam pressed against her back. It took three mule drivers to lift the beam and move it out of the way.

"Mama-san! Mama-san!" Ninepence and Less cried, falling to their knees beside Ai-weh-deh. The small woman did not move. Ninepence was scared; was Mama-san badly hurt? Was she . . . dead?

Then Ai-weh-deh rolled over slowly and sat up with a groan. "Ohh . . . my back," she moaned. She focused her eyes and looked at the frightened faces around her, then at the damaged room. "What happened? I—I heard a loud noise . . . and then the floor tilted and we all fell . . ."

Her voice died away as realization set in. "Yang! Hsi-Lien . . . and the others! We must help them!"

It seemed to take hours, but soon Ai-weh-deh, the
mule drivers, and the children had found Yang, Hsi-

Lien, and the other Christians who had been praying on the second floor. Everyone was bruised and sore, but miraculously, no one had been killed or seriously injured.

When everyone at the inn had been accounted for, Ai-weh-deh said, "Yang, stay here with the children. See if you can give them something to eat. Hsi-Lien, you and the other mule drivers come with me. We must go see what has happened . . . people will need help."

It was late when Ai-weh-deh and the mule drivers returned. Ninepence heard their voices out in the courtyard and rolled over on the cold *k'ang* where she and the other children had fallen asleep.

Trying not to wake the younger ones, Ninepence crawled off the *k'ang* and tiptoed to the damaged door.

"How bad?" Yang was asking anxiously.

"Very bad," said Ai-weh-deh. She sounded exhausted. "Many were killed or wounded by the explosions because everyone ran out into the streets to see the airplanes. We pulled many others out of the wreckage of the buildings, but . . . some may still be buried beneath the rubble."

Hsi-Lien spoke up. "The Mandarin has organized a relief committee—"

"Who?" Yang interrupted.

"Why, the Mandarin himself, and the prison governor, and a merchant named Lu Tchen, and of course Ai-weh-deh," the mule driver said.

"Oh, *of course* they would pick Ai-weh-deh," Yang muttered. "Does it matter that the house fell on her? That she has twenty-five children to care for? That she needs food and rest?"

"It's all right, Yang," Ninepence heard Ai-weh-deh say. "The relief committee will only organize what must be done . . . but it will take *everyone* who can stand and walk to help bury the dead and care for the wounded tomorrow—even the children. So let's get some food and rest if we can . . . do you have any soup left, Yang? We're famished!"

Chapter 10

Two Caves on the Mountain

LESS AND NINEPENCE CARRIED the pail of hot water between them to the cleared area where the wounded were being brought. Without a word, Ai-weh-deh took a bottle out of her pocket and poured some strong-smelling antiseptic into the steaming water. Wringing out a clean rag, she bent down beside a small child of about six who was sitting, dazed and speechless, in the dust.

After cleaning the long, jagged cut on the child's forehead and wrapping a clean bandage around it, Ai-weh-deh picked up the child and handed him to Less. "Take him back to the Inn of Eight Happinesses," she said wearily. "His father was killed by the bomb . . . and his mother just died of her wounds."

As Less and Ninepence started back to the inn

with the little boy, carefully picking their way around ruined homes and shops, they passed a line of prisoners carrying shovels.

"There's Feng!" said Ninepence, pointing excitedly. She waved at the prisoner who had been helping Ai-weh-deh organize work for the inmates at the prison. "What are you doing, Feng?"

"Digging graves outside the city walls," Feng called back, shaking his head sadly. "So many dead . . . so many . . ."

Less and Ninepence watched as the prisoners marched through the gate with their shovels, then took their young charge back to the inn.

By the end of the second day, ten more children orphaned by the bombs had been brought to the inn. Less, Ninepence, and the older children were kept busy carrying hot water and clean cloth to be ripped into bandages to Ai-weh-deh . . . helping Yang feed and comfort the children who had lost their parents . . . and trying to clean up some of the bomb damage in the main room of the inn.

That night a meeting of the relief committee was held in the courtyard of the Inn of Eight Happinesses. Ninepence hardly recognized the Mandarin, who had taken off his rich, long robe and put on the common blue coat and trousers of a working man to supervise searching the rubble for the dead and wounded. Only his sculptured mustache, long pigtail, and decisive manner distinguished him from the exhausted citizens of Yangcheng.

Yang, Hsi-Lien and his muleteers, and some of

the older children stood in the shadows, listening. "I have upsetting news," the Mandarin said wearily. "The Japanese have captured Luan and are marching on Tsehchow. It will be only a matter of days before their army arrives at the gates of Yangcheng. We must evacuate the city as soon as possible."

"But . . . how?" asked Ai-weh-deh. "Many are wounded and cannot walk."

"How many days do we have before the soldiers arrive, Excellency?" asked Lu-Tchen, the merchant. "Four? Five? We can send runners to the mountain villages and ask people to come take their wounded relatives home with them."

"Good idea!" said the Mandarin. "Everyone else must leave the city as soon as possible. Most of us have relatives in other villages."

The Governor of the Prison had been quiet to this point. "But what about my prisoners?" he asked. "We can't leave them here—the enemy will surely kill them."

Everyone was silent for a moment.

"You must release them," said Ai-weh-deh finally.

"*Release them?*"

"Yes. Send word to their relatives. The relatives must come and get them, and sign a paper saying that they are responsible."

"But—"

"Ai-weh-deh is right," agreed the Mandarin. "We cannot leave even prisoners to be slaughtered like hogs in a hog pen."

So it was decided. The town crier was sent

throughout the streets of Yangcheng, urging everyone to leave the city as soon as possible. Runners were sent to all the mountain villages, asking relatives to come collect their wounded and prisoners. Hsi-Lien, the mule driver, said goodbye to Ai-weh-deh and started back down the mule track toward his own village to see if his wife and children were all right.

At the Inn of Eight Happinesses, Ai-weh-deh decided they and the children would head for Bei Chai Chuang, a small mountain village perched high on the back of a mountain south of Yangcheng. Ai-weh-deh had been there before in her role as official Foot Inspector, and the people had asked her to return and tell them more Bible stories.

"I don't think they meant 'return with thirty-five children,'" Yang said wryly.

Ai-weh-deh smiled. "The Bible says, 'Whoever receives one of these little ones in my name receives Me.' We will give these good people an opportunity to 'receive Jesus' into their village, eh, Yang?"

Yang was silent a moment. "Ai-weh-deh?" he said. "I am not going with you. I am too old to climb the mountains anymore. If Yangcheng can no longer be my home, I am going back to my old village."

Ai-weh-deh's eyes filled with tears. "I—I understand, Yang. But . . . I will miss you. You have been a good friend . . . *more* than a friend. You have been like a father to me. I will never forget you." And, ignoring Chinese manners, she gave the old man a big hug.

The sun had not yet risen when Ai-weh-deh woke all the children the next day and told them to get ready: they were leaving at first light for Bei Chai Chuang. Ninepence was assigned to make sure each child had a bowl and a pair of chopsticks tied on their bundle, which included a change of clothes and a blanket. She was helping Bao-Bao tie his bundle across his back, when someone knocked loudly on the gate. Less opened it, and the Governor of the Prison rushed in, asking, "Where's Ai-weh-deh?" Feng was right behind him.

"What is it, Honorable Governor?" said Ai-weh-deh, stepping out of the inn with a small child strapped to her back and another on her hip.

"Ai-weh-deh, you must help!" cried the prison governor. "Feng . . . he has no relatives to sign for him."

"But what can I do?" cried Ai-weh-deh, looking around at the swarm of children staring sleepily at Feng and the governor.

"You must sign for him . . . he must go with you. There is no other way."

Ai-weh-deh stared helplessly at the young man.

Feng broke the awkward silence. "If you will sign for me, Ai-weh-deh, I will help with the children. You could use a man along. You have been a friend to me . . . now you will see, I will be a friend to you."

Ai-weh-deh smiled . . . and then she started to laugh. "If only my old friends in England could see me now. My Chinese 'family' consists of thirty-five children and a convict! Someone told me I must be crazy to want to be a missionary in China . . . and I guess it's true!" She held out her hand to Feng. "Yes, yes . . . I will sign for you."

When she had signed the paper, she said, "Now, come on, children, line up! Big boys and girls, take a little one by the hand. We are ready to leave. Okay now, let's sing. . . .

> *Count your blessings,*
> *Name them one by one. . . .*

The little band reached Bei Chai Chuang before dark. To most of the children it was a lark . . . especially when they left the mule trail and hiked up, up the mountain over rocky ground. When they stopped to eat from the pot of cold millet mush that some of the older boys had been carrying between them, the children acted as if they were having a picnic.

As Ai-weh-deh had predicted, the villagers of Bei Chai Chuang welcomed the strange little band. They listened in horror to the story of the Japanese bombs falling on Yangcheng, and the village elders put their heads together to figure out how to shelter and feed the refugees.

Because Bei Chai Chuang was built on the slope of a mountain, many of the farmers used natural caves to stable their animals. Two of the farmers offered to picket their animals outside and clean out the caves for Ai-weh-deh and her children to use. Feng and the older boys went right to work, and that night the children rolled out their blankets on beds of clean, sweet straw, the girls in one cave and the boys in the other. Ninepence fell asleep with shadows from a small, flickering fire dancing on the walls of the cave.

One week went by. Ai-weh-deh organized the children to help the villagers—weeding the small, rocky plots of millet, corn, and linseed, feeding the hogs, rounding up the few cows for milking, and watching the sheep graze on the tough, mountain grass. The villagers in turn shared their meager supply of food with their unexpected guests, and gathered each evening to hear Ai-weh-deh tell Bible stories about Jesus and Noah and Moses and Paul.

One evening, Ninepence was trying to coax a reluctant sheep to return to the village, when she saw a lone figure climbing the mountain. It looked like a man . . . wearing a uniform.

"Mama-san! Mama-san, come quickly!" she called, forgetting the sheep and scampering as quickly as she could over the rocky slopes to the cave in the side of the mountain. "Someone is coming!"

Ai-weh-deh followed Ninepence back to where she had first seen the man. He was much closer now, and he looked up and saw them.

Ai-weh-deh sucked in her breath. "It's Linnan!"

It took only a few more minutes for Colonel Linnan to finish climbing up the last slope. To

Ninepence's astonishment, the young army officer did not stop and bow politely as he usually did when he came to visit Ai-weh-deh. Instead, he covered the last few feet with big strides, took Ai-weh-deh in his arms and held her tightly.

"Oh, Ai-weh-deh . . . Ai-weh-deh!" he murmured. "I was so frightened when I heard about the bombing . . . ."

Ai-weh-deh seemed to rest a moment in Colonel Linnan's embrace . . . then she stepped back, her face flushed with pleasure. The colonel took Ninepence's hand and the three of them walked back toward the caves.

"When I heard that the Japanese had bombed Yangcheng, I came as quickly as I could," said Colonel Linnan, "but by then the Japanese army had occupied the town. I hid in the mountains until they left a few days later . . . but Yangcheng was totally deserted. I didn't know if you were alive or dead! I kept asking at the surrounding villages, and finally someone told me you and the children had come here to Bei Chai Chuang."

Feng's eyebrows went up when Ai-weh-deh said Colonel Linnan had arrived and would be staying for supper. The older boys took great interest in asking the army officer questions about the war. Who was winning? Could they fight, too? Would the Japanese come back to Yangcheng?

Laughing, Colonel Linnan finally dismissed the children and pulled Ai-weh-deh out into the mountain twilight for a walk. When they returned, most of

the children were asleep, and Ai-weh-deh and the
colonel sat by the fire to talk. Ninepence pretended

to be asleep, but she strained her ears to listen.

"Yes, Linnan, I do love you," Ai-weh-deh was saying, "and . . . I want to marry you, too. But . . ."

"But what? We could go to the Christian mission in Tsehchow and ask Reverend David Davis to marry us."

There was a long silence. The firelight flickered on the walls of the cave. Ninepence held her breath.

"No," Ai-weh-deh said finally. "Don't you see? We can't be together during the war. I am responsibile for all these children . . . and you have your duty. Everything is in crisis right now. We need time to think this through."

"Is it because you are English and I am Chinese?" asked Linnan. There was an edge to his voice.

"Oh, no!" said Ai-weh-deh. "I would be proud to be your wife. But . . . I am a Christian."

"Of course you are!" said Linnan. "I respect your beliefs. I am very interested in your God."

"I know, but . . ." Ai-weh-deh sighed. "We will talk about it again—after the war."

Ninepence thought the conversation was over. But after a few minutes Colonel Linnan spoke up again. "Ai-weh-deh, I want to ask a favor of you. Will you report to me anything you see about the movement of Japanese troops—and also the Chinese Communists?"

"Me? Spy?" cried Ai-weh-deh, raising her voice. "But I am a Christian! God's Son died for all people— even the Japanese. I cannot take sides in this war . . . I must remain neutral."

"Neutral!" said Linnan. The edge had returned to his cultured voice. "I am only trying to save the lives of my people . . . *your* people, Ai-weh-deh. You are a Chinese citizen, after all. Please think about it. I am not asking you to do something against your conscience—only to pass on information."

"All right," Ai-weh-deh promised. "I'll think about it."

There was a rustling at the front of the cave as Colonel Linnan left to go sleep in the boys' cave. Ai-weh-deh crept into the cave and lay down among the warm, sprawled bodies of the girls cuddled together.

But Ninepence stared at the shadows flickering on the cave walls for a long time.

Chapter 11

One Hundred Dollars Reward!

W HEN NINEPENCE WOKE UP the next morning, Colonel Linnan was gone.

But that same day they had another visitor. No one could approach Bei Chai Chuang without being seen. But Ninepence was surprised when one of the villagers brought a man to Ai-weh-deh just as the missionary was dividing the pot of millet and vegetables among thirty-eight bowls. At first Ninepence thought the man was a stranger. He looked old and broken; his mouth hung open and his eyes stared vacantly at nothing in particular. Still, there was something familiar about him. . . .

"Ai-weh-deh?" said the man in a hoarse whisper. "They're . . . they're all gone."

"Hsi-Lien!" cried Ai-weh-deh, recognizing her old

friend, the mule driver. "What has happened? Is it
your family? . . . Less! Get Hsi-Lien something to
eat."

The mule driver did not seem to notice the food
set down in front of him. It took constant prodding on
Ai-weh-deh's part, but gradually his story came out.

After Hsi-Lien had left Yangcheng and returned

to Chowtsun, his own village, he had found his wife and three children well. But a few days later, a Japanese patrol surprised them at supper and took Hsi-Lien outside. When they found out he was a mule driver, they said, "You are strong and know these mountains. You will carry our ammunition; if you do well, no harm will come to your family."

"But I cannot!" Hsi-Lien had cried. "I am a Christian now; I cannot fight and kill my brothers—*or* my enemies. If I carried your bullets, I would be helping you kill my own people. I—I cannot do it."

The Japanese soldiers were furious. But instead of killing Hsi-Lien, they tied him to a post in front of his own house. Then they locked his wife and children inside the house and set it on fire. . . .

Ninepence put her hands over her ears and ran back inside the cave. She didn't want to hear any more! That night she cried herself to sleep, crying for poor Hsi-Lien's innocent children, burned to death because their father was a Christian.

"It's too hard to be a Christian," Ninepence told Less the next day as they watched Ai-weh-deh, Hsi-Lien, Feng, and two strong farmers from Bei Chai Chuang head down the mountain toward Chowtsun to give Hsi-Lien's family a decent burial. "I couldn't do what Hsi-Lien did. I would have carried their stupid ammunition."

"I know," said Less. "But . . . the soldiers might have killed Hsi-Lien and his family anyway. Feng says that's the way war is."

When Ai-weh-deh, Feng, and the farmers returned, Hsi-Lien was still with them. "We are his family now," Feng told the children, putting his arm around the former mule driver, who still seemed half-crazy with shock and grief. "I will take care of him like my own brother."

But Ai-weh-deh had news for everyone. "The Nationalist soldiers have driven the Japanese out of Yangcheng. The Mandarin has already returned . . . and we have imposed on the good people of Bei Chai Chuang long enough." She looked around at Feng and all the children. "So . . . I think we should go back to the Inn of Eight Happinesses and help our fellow citizens rebuild our city. What do you think?"

"Hooray!" yelled Less. He was getting tired of chasing sheep and cows over the steep slopes of the mountain.

"Hooray!" yelled the other children. The adventure of living in caves had worn off and they were eager to go back home, where they could have a nice, warm *k'ang* to sleep on.

"Me too?" said Bao-Bao, pointing to himself. Everybody laughed.

Only Feng had misgivings about going back to Yangcheng. "Will I be put back in the prison again, Ai-weh-deh?" he asked gravely.

"No, no," Ai-weh-deh assured him. "I have signed for you; you are my responsibility now, and I will not let you go back."

The Inn of Eight Happinesses just wasn't the same without Yang. Feng did his best to learn how to cook, but the millet mush was often scorched, the vegetables raw, the dough strings . . . well, too stringy. Sometimes Ninepence thought she could do a better job than he did feeding their large family.

Only about half the people returned to Yang-cheng, so rebuilding was slow. Some thought it was a waste of time. "Those planes might come again and drop their bombs, and it would all be for nothing!" they grumbled. Also, working in the fields to grow food took priority over rebuilding the town.

The second floor of the inn, however, got repaired with the help of Feng, Hsi-Lien, and some of the Mandarin's men. A few mule trains came along the mule track and some of the drivers stayed at the inn, but business was down. With the city of Luan to the north in enemy hands, the flow of goods over the mountains had slowed to a trickle.

Sometimes Nationalist soldiers came to Yang-cheng with news of the war. Tsehchow had fallen to the Japanese . . . then the Nationalists had taken it back again. Most of the battles were being fought down in the valleys, and Yangcheng seemed fairly safe . . . for now.

Ai-weh-deh resumed some of her trips to the sur-rounding villages, but not in her old role as official Foot Inspector. There was no time to enforce the new law now . . . but she did want to encourage the little groups of Christians that had sprung up not only in Yangcheng but also in Bei Chai Chuang, Chowtsun, and some of the other mountain villages.

Ninepence decided that wasn't all Ai-weh-deh was doing on these trips. When she returned, Ninepence saw her writing notes addressed to Colonel Linnan, Nationalist Army, Tsehchow. Had Ai-weh-deh decided to spy for the colonel after all?

Ninepence didn't have much time to think about these notes, however, because more often than not, Ai-weh-deh also returned from these trips with another child or two, orphaned by the fierce fighting between Chinese and Japanese, or Nationalist Chinese and Communist Chinese. As summer faded to fall, and fall slipped into winter, more and more children arrived at the Inn of Eight Happinesses. Ai-weh-deh's attitude seemed to be, "There's already too many, so what's one more—or ten? God will provide . . . somehow."

But it was a hard winter. Each older child was paired with a younger child—or two or three—to care for. The townspeople shared what food they could. But Ninepence and the other children often went to sleep with only a small bowl of millet mush to fill their tummies.

Still, no one complained about the cold and snow that kept them cooped up inside the Inn of Eight Happinesses. At least the snow had closed the mountain passes and shut out the Japanese army. For the first time since the bombs had dropped, everyone in Yangcheng relaxed and felt safe.

As warm spring breezes melted the snow in the mountains of southern Shansi, news traveled up the mule track: the Japanese were advancing! The citizens of Yangcheng panicked, and fled for the mountain villages. Ai-weh-deh and her growing brood of children, along with Feng and Hsi-Lien, hiked up the mountain to Bei Chai Chuang and stayed in the caves until the danger was past. Then, once again, the Japanese were driven out and people trickled back into Yangcheng to patch their lives back together again.

That winter there were even more mouths to feed at the Inn of Eight Happinesses, but at least the snows gave them a measure of safety. Sometimes Ninepence, now twelve years old, lay on one of the *k'angs* at night, scrunched between Tiger Lily or Crystal or one of the newer girls, trying to remember what life had been like "before the bomb." She missed old Yang . . . and she missed the dough strings and chicken soup and sweet cakes he used to make. Now it was millet mush, day after day after day. . . .

As the spring of 1940 thawed the mule track, one night there was a loud knock at the courtyard gate. Less, now fifteen, ran to see who it was.

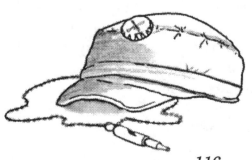

"It's Colonel Linnan to see you, Mama-san!" he said, running into the inn. The handsome army officer didn't wait on ceremony but followed Less right into the room where Ai-weh-deh was helping some of the younger children get ready for bed.

"Ai-weh-deh," he said urgently, "I have come to see the Mandarin . . . but first I must see you—alone."

Ai-weh-deh seemed pleased to see him. "Alone?" she laughed, tipping her chin at the roomful of children. "Easier said than done, Linnan." But after asking Feng to tell that night's Bible story, Ai-weh-deh and Colonel Linnan went out into the slushy courtyard, closing the door behind them. They were still in the courtyard, their voices rising and falling sharply, when Feng turned down the lamps and told the children to go to sleep.

The next morning Ai-weh-deh seemed upset as she spooned up the millet mush. Ninepence watched anxiously as her adopted mother gave some children a second spoonful while skipping others entirely.

"Let me do that," Ninepence said suddenly, taking the spoon out of Ai-weh-deh's hand. When all the children had something in the bottom of their bowls, the young girl pulled Ai-weh-deh aside. "What did Colonel Linnan want, Mama-san?" she asked boldly. "Are you . . . are you going to marry him and go away from us?"

"Oh, Ninepence!" said Ai-weh-deh, touching the girl's face gently. "I would never leave you! You are my adopted daughter, remember? Colonel Linnan just . . . just had some news about the war. I—I need to think about what to do. Don't worry about it . . . all right?"

Ninepence nodded and Ai-weh-deh gave her a quick hug. But as the small woman hurried off to supervise morning chores, a piece of paper fell out of her trouser pocket and fluttered to the floor. Ninepence quickly snatched it up.

"ONE HUNDRED DOLLARS REWARD!" the paper said across the top. Then more words: "One hundred dollars reward will be paid by the Japanese army for information leading to the capture—alive—of . . ." Here the paper listed three names. The first two names were men Ninepence had never heard of. But her heart nearly stopped when she read the third name:

"Gladys Aylward, known as Ai-weh-deh."

Chapter 12

Over the Mountains

NINEPENCE WANTED TO TALK to Ai-weh-deh about the paper, but she was afraid. Then a messenger from the Mandarin arrived at the Inn of Eight Happinesses, breathless and agitated. "The Japanese are preparing a major assault! Colonel Linnan has brought an order from the Nationalist High Commander: a 'scorched earth' policy!"

" 'Scorched earth'?" said Feng, bewildered, as the children clustered wide-eyed in the courtyard with Ai-weh-deh and Hsi-Leng to hear the news. "What does that mean?"

"We must burn our crops! Tear the roofs from our houses! Flee—but leave no food or shelter for the invaders. It will slow them down. That's an order."

"Mama-san—look!" cried Less, pointing to the sky. Smoke was rising beyond the walls of Yangcheng. Several of the older boys ran up to the second-floor balcony to see what it was. "It's the Nationalist soldiers . . . burning the crops!" Less called down to the upturned faces below.

The messenger turned back to Ai-weh-deh. "Yes, the destruction has already begun. You must get ready to leave tomorrow."

"But . . . where will we go?" asked Ai-weh-deh. "I have nearly a hundred children here! We are far too many to hide in the caves of Bei Chai Chuang."

"No, no!" said the messenger. "That is too close. The Mandarin said to tell you that Madame Chiang Kai-Shek, the wife of the Nationalist General, has set up orphanages in Sian. That is where you must take the children."

"Sian!" exclaimed Ai-weh-deh. "But . . . that is in the next province . . . over the mountains . . . beyond the Yellow River!"

"Yes, yes!" said the messenger. "But there you will be safe." He turned to go. "Oh . . . one other thing. The Mandarin wishes to say goodbye before you leave. Will you please come to a feast at the *yamen* tonight? You and your three adopted children are invited."

"Yes . . . yes, of course," said Ai-weh-deh, absently. She stood with her eyes closed for a few minutes. Ninepence noticed how tired her adopted mother looked.

But then Ai-weh-deh squared her shoulders and took a deep breath. "Come on, children . . . we're going on an adventure—over the mountains! Less, you and the boys get up there and ruin the roof! Ninepence . . . Tiger Lily . . . Glorious Ruby . . . all you older girls—help me pack. Every child must have a blanket, an extra jacket, a pair of shoes, a bowl, and chopsticks in their pack . . ."

Less, Ninepence, and Bao-Bao were so excited at being invited to the Mandarin's house for a farewell feast that they could hardly eat. Ai-weh-deh was the only woman present . . . but she sat in the seat of honor next to the Mandarin. The Governor of the Prison was there, Lu-Tchen and several other important merchants, government officials, as well as Colonel Linnan and several other army officers.

The "feast," however, was quite simple: stewed fruit and bread, fish, bowls of millet, peanuts, and tea—nice, but not quite what Ninepence had imagined. "It's because of the war, silly," whispered Less. "Nobody has expensive food anymore—not even the Mandarin."

After the meal, the Mandarin stood and held a hand up for silence. "I asked you all to this feast tonight to say goodbye," he said, his voice full of emotion, "but also to honor a very special person. We all know Ai-weh-deh, who was first known to us as Gladys Aylward . . . ."

Ai-weh-deh looked down at her lap, embarrassed. Less grinned and poked Ninepence.

"She has functioned well in her role as my official Foot Inspector," the Mandarin went on, "which she did while running a popular inn for mule drivers— very essential to the economy of our city. Along the way, she and I have had many long conversations about Christianity, the faith that she says brought her to China in the first place. I think we have all seen this faith in action as she has cared for our poor and our sick . . . helped our prison become a more humane place for the prisoners . . . and mothered countless orphans."

Heads all around the table were nodding respect-fully.

"There is no way I can adequately thank you, Ai-weh-deh," said the Mandarin, looking directly at her, "except . . . I would like to share your faith, Ai-weh-deh. I want to become a Christian."

Ai-weh-deh's eyes flew up, and her mouth dropped open in shock. "Y-Your Excellency," she stammered, "I . . . hardly know what to say, except . . . that I am glad. Oh, yes, I am so glad!"

Seven-year-old Bao-Bao fell asleep against Ninepence as talk turned to the approaching Japa-nese and how best to evacuate the city. The children waited as Ai-weh-deh had a private conversation with the Mandarin after the other guests had left. When they finally left the *yamen* to walk home,

Ninepence was surprised to see Colonel Linnan still waiting for them.

"Ai-weh-deh," the colonel said, his young, handsome face lined with worry, "have you reconsidered my offer? It is my fault that the Japanese are looking for you! But my soldiers would protect you and take you to safety."

Tears welled up in Ai-weh-deh's eyes. "Thank you, Linnan. I—I know your only thought is my safety. But . . ." She pulled Bao-Bao and Ninepence closer as Less stood close by protectively. ". . . *my* responsibility is to these children. I could never put my own safety first."

Colonel Linnan swallowed hard, as if he was having trouble speaking. "I know," he said in a hoarse whisper. "But I'm afraid . . . this might be goodbye."

No one spoke. The stars had come out, and the night over Yangcheng was quiet and peaceful. Colonel Linnan took Ai-weh-deh's hand in his and kissed it gently. The next moment he was gone.

The long line of children snaked along the trail used by the mule trains to cross the mountains into Shansi, the next province. The April sun felt warm on their bare heads, and the little ones scampered over the rocks like excited rabbits.

The Mandarin had donated two big bags of millet for the trip, and two men to carry them partway. Feng carried a big iron pot to cook the millet, and Ai-weh-deh had tucked a precious supply of matches and hot twig tea into her pack. But it had been apparent that Hsi-Lien was not strong enough to make the trip; the Mandarin, now a believer, had agreed to take the unfortunate mule driver with him to his ancestral village.

As the sun disappeared behind the mountains at the end of the first day, many of the littlest children were being carried piggyback by the older ones.

"Where are we going to sleep, Ninepence?" asked Bao-Bao, looking around fearfully at the lengthening shadows. He had heard many tales from the mule drivers about the bandits that lived in the mountains.

"Ai-weh-deh said there is a village up ahead, about one day's walk from Yangcheng. Maybe they will give us shelter there," said Ninepence. She too was thinking about the bandits.

Just then word came back along the line: "The

village! It's just around the next bend!"

The village was like many others tucked away in the mountains. Most of the people farmed little plots tucked into the ravines and carved from the mountain slopes. This village also had its own Buddhist temple, and it was here that the children were invited to spend the night. Tired from their long day's hike, they sprawled over the temple floor like little rag dolls and immediately fell asleep.

The next day the hardy shrubs along the mule track gave way to a thick forest. The older boys, impatient with the slow progress of the little ones, ran ahead, marking the trail for the others to follow.

Soon the cheerful enthusiasm of the morning gave way to complaints of "I'm tired, Ai-weh-deh . . . can't we

rest now?" and "Are we almost there?"

"No, no . . . we have many days to go," said Ai-weh-deh. "But come on, now, let's sing! That will give us some energy to go a few more miles. Listen . . . I will teach you a new song."

Soon the melody of "We're marching to Zion, beautiful, beautiful Zion" was bouncing off the mountainsides in youthful Chinese voices.

That night there was no village, so Ai-weh-deh, Feng, and the children rolled up in their blankets and slept in the open. Again, tired from the daylong hike, the children immediately fell into a deep slumber.

Three days passed, then four, falling into a familiar routine. Usually the morning started out with games of tag and cheerful squeals ringing out along the trail. When the sun was high overhead, Ai-weh-deh blew her whistle to call everyone together to eat their midday meal, cooked in the big iron pot. Then, as the shadows got longer, many of the little children needed to be carried. At this point, Less and a couple of the bigger boys hiked on ahead, scouting for a place to spend the night. Sometimes a sympathetic villager would let them sleep in his courtyard; other nights they spent under the stars on the mountainsides.

But on the fifth day, the Mandarin's millet ran out and his two helpers turned back. And on the sixth day, there was no village from which to beg food. That night the children rolled up in their blankets, with only a drink from a mountain creek to fill their bellies.

As Ninepence huddled in her blanket close to Tiger Lily, with Precious Pearl's warm breath on the back of her neck, she could see Ai-weh-deh still sitting by their cooking fire. And then she heard a familiar melody lulling them to sleep. . . .

> *Count your blessings,*
> *Name them one by one.* . . .

"What blessings?" Ninepence muttered to herself, shifting her hips away from a sharp rock poking through her blanket. "Blisters on my feet, no supper, sunburn on my nose . . . and now it's beginning to rain!"

The next day all the children were damp, hungry, and cranky. Ninepence felt irritated by Tiger Lily and Bao-Bao, one of whom always seemed to be tagging along with her. "Leave me alone!" she finally snapped and stalked off through the scrubby bushes.

Leaving the trail, the twelve-year-old scrambled higher up the rocky mountainside and then leveled off, trying to keep parallel with the trail below. *This is great!* she decided. As one of the "older" girls, she seldom had a moment to herself. She was always wiping noses, kissing a scraped knee, or telling the story of Noah and the animals—for the zillionth time.

The day began cloudy after the nighttime shower, but the sun broke through. Ninepence half closed her eyes, soaking up the welcome warmth on her damp jacket. She could hear the whimpers of the tired children down below, but she felt far removed from the ragged line strung out for hundreds of yards.

From up above, she could see far down the trail, winding in and out of boulders, scrub bushes, and hardy spruce and fir trees. As she drank in the peaceful landscape, a movement along the trail ahead caught her eye. Had some of the older boys run that far ahead? she wondered. But no, she could almost make out the small figures now . . . there were at least twenty people on the trail coming *toward* them.

Then the sun glinted off something metal . . . lots of metal . . . and the mountain breeze carried the unmistakable whinny of a horse.

Ninepence's mouth went dry.

Soldiers! Ai-weh-deh and the other children were walking straight into the arms of enemy soldiers!

Chapter 13

Walking on Water

NINEPENCE QUICKLY CROUCHED LOW and began to slide down the rocky slope toward the trail. Her hands stung as she grabbed prickly scrub branches to keep from falling on the way down.

A cascade of small, loose rocks and pebbles preceded her. "Ninepence!" Ai-weh-deh started to scold. "Where have you been—"

"Soldiers, Mama-san!" she cried, trying to whisper. "Up ahead! I saw them!"

Immediately Ai-weh-deh began to run, trying to alert the children who were walking ahead of her. Ninepence ran down the

line, whispering hoarsely, "Hide! Soldiers ahead! Hide! Hide!"

A three-year-old girl saw the bigger children scattering off the trail and let out a frightened cry. Ninepence grabbed the little girl and clapped a hand over her mouth. "Hush! Hush!" she hissed in the child's ear, scrambling awkwardly over the rocks toward a little clump of fir trees.

They reached the trees and fell down on the ground, along with five or six other children who were huddled together beneath the branches. Ninepence's heart was beating wildly. *So many children can never hide from the soldiers!* she thought frantically. *Some little one will cry out . . . someone will be seen!* In desperation, she kept her hand pressed over the little girl's mouth as the child's chest heaved with silent sobs.

Then she heard Ai-weh-deh's voice calling. "Children! Children! It's all right . . . you can come out now. Some Nationalist soldiers have found us!"

With cries of relief and joy, children spilled from behind every tree and large rock along the trail for hundreds of yards. Ninepence took her hand away from the little girl's mouth, and the child angrily balled her hand into a fist and tried to hit Ninepence, then ran after the others.

As Ninepence walked back toward the children and soldiers, she felt embarrassed. She had scared everyone, and it was only Nationalist soldiers.

"You are going all the way to Sian . . . with all these children?" the officer in charge asked in astonishment. "But that is still many days—"

"Yes, yes, we are going to Sian," interrupted Ai-weh-deh impatiently. "But right now we need food. All the children are very hungry. Can you help us?"

The officer barked an order, and in a few moments the soldiers were unbuckling their packs and sharing their rations of peanuts, while the army cook boiled up a big pot of millet. Soon the children were holding out their bowls for the familiar food.

Ninepence hung back, still embarrassed at her false alarm. But Ai-weh-deh bent close to her ear and said, "Ninepence, you did exactly the right thing. In wartime, a person can't be too careful. I'm proud of you. Now get your ration . . . go on! Go on!"

The sack of millet that the soldiers gave Ai-weh-deh lasted another four days—but only because one night Feng could find no water to cook it in. And by the twelfth day away from Yangcheng, the state of the children's health was getting serious.

Like the others, Ninepence's thin, cloth shoes had long since worn out, and she stumbled along the mule track on blistered, swollen feet. There was very little singing now; the constant hours under the sun had burned her face and cracked her lips, and her tongue felt thick and cottony with thirst. Her clothes and hair were matted with dirt, but she didn't care. All she wanted was to get to the river . . . the river . . .

And then the cry traveled hoarsely back along

the line: "The river! The Yellow River!"

Sure enough, as the line of children snaked down along the foothills, they could see the town of Yuan Ku below them, and beyond the town, a long ribbon of water sparkling in the distance.

Excitement overcame exhaustion and blisters. Water, food, and shelter were just a few miles away! Childish voices spontaneously sang, "Count your blessings, name them one by one. . . ."

But as they entered the town of Yuan Ku, it was strangely quiet and empty. Many houses and other buildings were in ruins; rubble littered the streets.

"Hello? Anybody here?" hollered Feng as he pounded on first one courtyard gate and then another. But there was no answer, not even a yapping dog.

The entire town was deserted.

Several of the children began to cry with disappointment and hunger. Even Ai-weh-deh had trouble speaking. "Never mind," she said finally. "We'll go on to the river. Boys over ten . . . search the empty houses, see what you can find to eat. Everyone else, come on now . . . we've made it over the mountains; we can make it to the river."

The last three miles felt like torture to Ninepence. But when they reached the ferry landing on the bank of the immense river, she and the children fell into the shallows, laughing and splashing the cool water over their sunburned faces and blistered feet. The older boys found some moldy millet in one house, and some flat, hard bread left behind in a baker's shop. Feng boiled up the millet—more like a watery

soup than a thick mush—and small pieces of bread were dipped in it and given to the youngest children.

"But where is the ferry?" Less asked, shading his

eyes against the setting sun and looking up and down the empty river.

"Maybe we got here too late, and it's on the other side," suggested Ai-weh-deh. "Come on . . . let's have a Bible story and get some sleep. A boat will come tomorrow."

But the next day a boat did not come. And when still another day and night passed, Ai-weh-deh was clearly worried. Ninepence heard her tell Feng that it was obvious the Japanese had bombed Yuan Ku, and the people had fled across the river. But why didn't they send the ferry back for other refugees?

The older boys made two more trips back to Yuan Ku to search for food; the meager bits and pieces they found were all thrown in a pot, but the watery soup did little to satisfy the constant hunger in their bellies. As the sun hung low on the far side of the wide river for the third time, the children lay on the bank, too hungry and tired to play in the water. Ai-weh-deh paced up and down, scanning the horizon, but still no boat.

Something was bothering Ninepence. "Mamasan?" she asked. "Remember the story in the Bible you told us many times . . . about how Moses led the children of Israel right up to the banks of the Red Sea . . . with their enemies right behind chasing them?"

Ai-weh-deh frowned. "Yes, I remember."

"And God told Moses to command the river to open, and God's people walked across on dry ground?"

"Yes."

"Then . . . why doesn't God open the Yellow River

for us so we can go across?"

Ai-weh-deh was silent for a moment; then tears ran down her cheeks. "I am not Moses, Ninepence."

"But . . . God is God—you have told us so many times. If God is really God, *He* can get us across the river."

Again Ai-weh-deh was silent for a long time. Then she drew Ninepence to her and held her in her arms. "You are right, my sweet daughter. My faith has been so small . . . let us call all the children together, and we will pray."

Feng built up the fire and the children gathered around. Ai-weh-deh once more told the story of Moses and the Red Sea, and then she prayed. And one by one, many of the children prayed, too.

"Please, God, send us a boat," said Tiger Lily.

"God, could You push back the water and make a mule track for us in the sand?" Ninepence prayed.

"Or maybe we could walk on *top* of the water, like Jesus did!" piped up Bao-Bao, squinching his eyes.

"Thank You, God, that we all made it across the mountains safely," prayed Less. "If it's not too much to ask, we would like to get across the river, too."

Hardly anyone felt like sleeping. So Ai-weh-deh told them another Bible story . . . and another. And in between they sang, "Jesus Loves Me" . . . "This Little Light of Mine" . . . and "Trust and Obey."

Suddenly a strange figure walked into the firelight.

"A soldier!" someone screamed.

Startled, Ai-weh-deh stood up. For the first time

Ninepence noticed how thin her adopted mother had gotten, how she swayed as if she were going to fall over.

"Are you in charge here?" the soldier asked gruffly, looking the small woman up and down. Ninepence could see by his uniform that he was a Nationalist officer. "Who are you . . . and who are all these children?"

Ai-weh-deh replied politely that she was a missionary from Yangcheng, and she was taking all these children to an orphanage in Sian.

"You mean . . . you brought all these children over the mountains?" the man asked, astonished.

"Yes," she said wearily. "We are trying to cross the river to safety."

"But . . . don't you realize this area will soon be a battlefield?" the officer cried. "The Japanese bombers have already been here, and their army is on the march!"

Feng spoke up. "All the more reason we must get these children across the river! But . . . we have been here three days and no boats have come. What has happened?"

The officer shook his head. "The river has been closed by the Nationalist government. But . . . I think I can get a boat for you. However, you must realize you would be taking a great risk. If a Japanese plane should come while you were out in the open water . . ."

Ai-weh-deh swayed again. Alarmed, Less, Ninepence, and Bao-Bao rushed to her side, as if to prop her up.

"This woman is ill!" the officer said sternly to Feng. "You must see that she gets medical attention on the other side."

"No . . . I will be all right," said Ai-weh-deh, a faint smile lighting her exhausted face. "You see?" she said to the children, who all started to cluster around her. "God is going to get us across this Yellow 'Sea' . . . just like Moses and the children of Israel!"

"Except we're going on *top* of the water," Bao-Bao laughed.

The officer went to the ferry landing and blew sharply on a whistle three times. Hearing the whistle, the officer's men—a reconnaissance squad of eight young boys, only a few years older than Less—came out of the bushes where they had been told to hide until the officer discovered whether the campfire and singing was a Japanese trap. At the same time, a shout went up from the children: "The boat! The boat is coming!"

It was the boat that was going to pick up the officer and his squad after sundown, when the danger of Japanese planes flying low over the river was not as great. Surprised at seeing the bank full of children, the boatmen nonetheless loaded as many as possible into the boat and began rowing back across.

It took three trips to get all the children across. Feng went with the first boatload and waited on the other side as the children arrived. Ai-weh-deh went in the last boatload, along with Bao-Bao, Less, and Ninepence.

The last light was fading on the horizon as Ninepence watched the oars on the large rowboat dip up and down into the water. The province of Shansi was on the other side . . . and beyond that—still a walk of many days—was the city of Sian, their new home.

Behind them was Yangcheng and the Inn of Eight Happinesses . . . now only a bombed-out shell. Would they ever go home again? Something deep inside told Ninepence that they would never go back.

She leaned against Ai-weh-deh and realized that Bao-Bao had fallen asleep, his head in Ai-weh-deh's lap. "Mama-san," she whispered, not wanting to wake her little brother, "will you stay at the orphanage in Sian, too?"

Ai-weh-deh shook her head. "No, Ninepence. I came to China to share the Gospel . . . and my work is not yet done. I must visit the villages and tell the people the Good News about God's Son."

Ninepence sat up, alarmed, and looked in Ai-weh-deh's face. "But . . . what about us? Me, and Less, and Bao-Bao? Are you going to leave us?"

Ai-weh-deh smiled and shook her head again. "No, Ninepence. I will never leave you. You and Less and Bao-Bao are my very own adopted children. You will go with me wherever I go."

With a sigh, Ninepence relaxed against Ai-weh-deh once more and watched as the children on the far shore grew larger. *Now* she knew where "home" was going to be.

"Home" was wherever Ai-weh-deh was.

More About Gladys Aylward

GLADYS AYLWARD WAS BORN in February 1902, the daughter of a postman in a close-knit, happy family. Like many working-class English girls, she went into "service" as a parlormaid. But this parlormaid had a burning desire: to go to China as a missionary.

In 1928, at the age of twenty-six, she applied to the China Inland Mission. But after only three months of training, the principal suggested that she give up her hopes of going to China. Her grades were poor and by graduation she would be almost thirty. And the mission thought that only younger people could learn such a difficult language as Chinese.

Discouraged, Gladys became a "rescue sister," ministering to the prostitutes who hung around the Swansea docks in southern Wales. But the conviction that God had called her to China would not die. When she heard that an elderly missionary in China, named Jennie Lawson, wanted a young assistant, Gladys said, "That's me!" She went back to work as a parlormaid and saved her money to buy a one-way ticket to China.

Finally, on Saturday, October 15, 1932, Gladys bid farewell to her family and friends and set off by train that would cross England, Europe, Russia, and Siberia on her way to Tientsin, China, where she finally arrived nearly a month later.

Jennie Lawson was supposedly in Tsehchow (which means "the road ends here") in the province of Shansi, but when Gladys arrived by bus several weeks later, she discovered that Mrs. Lawson had moved to Yangcheng in the wild mountains two days farther west. The only way to get there was by mule.

When Gladys finally arrived in Yangcheng, she could hardly contain her joy that God had finally brought her to China. Jennie Lawson had purchased a ramshackle, old inn just outside the walls of the mountain town; her idea was to convert it into an inn for the muleteers and coolies driving the mule trains across the mountains with trade goods. Not only would the inn offer good food and a place to sleep, but the women would tell stories—Gospel stories.

When Gladys had been in Yangcheng only eight months, Jennie Lawson had an accident and died after an illness of several months. Income from the inn barely covered the overhead, so Gladys was grateful when the Mandarin of Yangcheng said he needed an official "Foot Inspector" because the ancient custom of binding the feet of all female children to keep their feet tiny had just been outlawed. The Mandarin decided that the foot inspector must be a woman with large feet—so he picked Gladys. Though her feet were only size three, they looked huge in comparison to the bound feet of Chinese women.

This turned out to be God's blessing for Gladys. The position not only gave her a small income but a mule and the authority to visit the mountain villages where she also told the villagers about Jesus.

During her second year in Yangcheng, Gladys helped quell a riot that broke out in the local prison, and afterward she worked hard for prison reform. After that, the people of the town quit calling her a "foreign devil," and instead called her "Ai-weh-deh," which means "the Virtuous One." After several years in Yangcheng, Gladys decided to become a Chinese citizen, to better identify with the people she loved.

The Mandarin also introduced her to Colonel Linnan, the handsome intelligence officer in the Nationalist army with whom Gladys fell in love.

Rumors of war between the Chinese and Japanese, and between the Nationalists and the Communists, were ignored by most peasants in the mountains. Who would bother these remote villages? But on a bright spring day in 1938, loud "silver birds" flew overhead. The people of Yangcheng ran out to see the strange sight—until the bombs exploded. The Japanese were bombing Yangcheng! War had arrived.

A pattern followed: the Japanese would bomb a

town or village, followed a few days later by their army moving in to occupy the town. But often they would find the town deserted because the people had fled into the mountains to hide. Then the Nationalist army would push the Japanese out, the people would return to bury their dead and rebuild their lives . . . and then the cycle would start over again.

During the war Gladys tried to be neutral; but when Colonel Linnan asked her to help China by passing along information she gathered in her visits to the villages, she became a spy, though she often struggled with her conscience about doing so.

In February 1940, Gladys visited David Davis, a fellow missionary, in Tsehchow, which was occupied by the Japanese. There she discovered two hundred war orphans. Although the Japanese generally left the mission alone, one day several soldiers crashed into the mission to rape the women. When Gladys tried to stop them, she was beaten to the ground, suffering internal injuries that plagued her for years.

When Gladys heard that Madame Chiang Kai-shek had started several orphanages for war orphans—one of which was in Sian, in the next province—she sent Tsin Pen Kuang, a Christian convert, across the mountains with a hundred children, whom he delivered safely. But on the return journey he was captured by the Japanese, so Gladys was left with getting the rest of the children out herself.

She sent the second "hundred" children from Tsehchow to Yangcheng with some Christian women. But the Japanese were coming closer. Then Gladys heard that the Japanese had put a price on her head for being a spy! As she ran from Tsehchow, a bullet grazed her right shoulder blade; but she got away and, after two days, finally reached Yangcheng and the Inn of Eight Happinesses.

Knowing she was "wanted" made Gladys determined to leave southern Shansi and take the children with her. The very next day she began the journey over the mountains with almost a hundred children, ages three to sixteen. After nearly a month of supreme effort and courage and depending on the providence of God, Gladys and every single one of the children finally arrived in Sian, where the children were cared for by Madame Chiang Kai-shek's "New Life" organization and sent to nearby Fufeng to an orphanage and school. It was April 1940.

But Gladys was weak and ill and ended up in a delirium, a combination of typhus and the internal injuries from the beating. Peasants took her to the Scandinavian-American Mission at Hsing P'ing and put her into the care of the senior physician there. After many weeks, she recovered but was still weak. She reclaimed her five adopted children, settling with her children in Baochi, in the westerly province of Chengtu, doing odd jobs to provide for them.

Colonel Linnan came to see her and again asked her to marry him, but this time she said no. Something had changed. She knew that she needed to be free to continue carrying the Gospel to the villages.

After twenty years in China, an American paid her fare for a visit (without her children) to England in

1942. However, while there the doors to China closed under Communist rule, so Gladys stayed until 1957. During this time Alan Burgess, a BBC writer and producer, met Gladys and wrote the book *The Small Woman*, on which the Hollywood movie *Inn of the Sixth Happiness*, starring Ingrid Bergman, was based.

On April 4, 1957, Gladys once again sailed for China, but this time to Hong Kong and Formosa. To her joy, she was reunited with a few of her adopted children, who by this time were married and had families of their own. However, Less had died, shot by the Communists when he refused to do something contrary to his beliefs. Others had been taken away to concentration camps or prison.

At age fifty-five, Gladys did not intend to get into orphan work again, but soon unwanted babies and children were showing up on her doorstep. She started the Gladys Aylward Orphanage in Formosa and soon had a hundred children.

It was here that Gladys Aylward, the "small woman" who was "unqualified" to be a missionary, served until her death in 1970.

For Further Reading

Burgess, Alan. *The Small Woman*. London: Evans Brothers Ltd., 1957, 1969.

"Inn of the Sixth Happiness" (movie/video), starring Ingrid Bergman. Based on *The Small Woman* by Alan Burgess.

Swift, Catherine. *Gladys Aylward*. Minneapolis: Bethany House Publishers, 1989.